DANCING

WITH

DRAGONFLIES

— ·· —

LAURA ADAMS

LAURA ADAMS

CHAPTER 1

—:—

MEL

Mel pulled her coat tightly around herself as the month of October nipped at her skin. Her breathe rose through the night air as if delivering a message to the invisible, while her coat pocket vibrated for the eighth time. She decided against answering, disinterested in the pleading that would follow if she did. Her mum, Grace, would be pacing the floor which is what she did when she was stressed, and while Mel felt bad about being the cause of that stress, she also needed some space to breathe. She had not expected to end up at her marital home when she went on a drive. The home she no longer lived in.

Sitting on the jetty looking out at the lake with the house behind her, Mel examined the blackness of the water below and found it hard to believe it was the same water she had swum in on hot summer days as a child. Now it looked ominous in the darkness of night. She'd been wrong. She'd thought coming here would feel familiar and safe but instead it felt remote and unsettling.

The night air forced her to her feet. Mel walked towards the house, as chills rippled through her, not related to the weather. She steadied herself as the key slipped into the lock.

The smell of the house hit her first, a mixture of vanilla and sandalwood. The smell of heartache, love, and dreams. Her boots echoing on the wood floor, a reminder that she was alone. She touched the fireplace surround and examined the film of dust that coated her finger like a second skin. Evidence of another lifetime when things were as they should have been.

Mel remembered standing in this very spot in front of a roaring fire that filled the room with warmth. The scent of cinnamon and oranges had hung in the air. She had sipped a sweet sherry, a drink she only ever indulged in on Christmas Eve, smiling as she looked at the presents stacked around the tree, while watching Carter build Ella's fairy castle, his brow had been furrowed as he tried to make sense of the instructions that had consisted of pictures.

The grandfather clock chimed, snapping her back to the present moment. Mel stumbled towards the sofa, exhausted. The need to curl up was overwhelming, so she pulled the sheet off and watched the dance of the dust motes illuminated by the moon. She wrapped the sheet tightly around herself and lay against the cold leather, remembering a time when she had lay on this very sofa with Ella when she was a baby. She had inhaled her milky sweetness and her tiny hand had clasped one of Mel's fingers, as if afraid to let her go. Mel wondered if she had held on to Ella a little tighter whether she would have still been alive. Closing her eyes, she welcomed the darkness that had stood by her side for the past eighteen months.

After a restless night she drifted into consciousness, blinking herself back to life as daylight streamed through the window. The memories of the previous day prickled her brain, and she sat upright, heart pounding. Her mum and sister would be frantic. Mel fumbled in her pocket for her phone. Thirty-six missed calls. Panic rose like a rogue wave as she called her sister.

'Mel, where the fuck are you?' said Ari. 'Why did you not call me back? I was so worried I called the police!'

'The police! That's a bit dramatic, isn't it?' Anger surged through Mel at the reminder that her life was no longer her own.

'Not really Mel, given how you've been the past...' Ari's voice trailed off.

'I'm sorry, okay? I just needed some space.'

She pictured her sister rubbing her temple, trying to massage the stress away. Her big sister who took it upon herself to look after her even though she didn't need a minder.

'I'm fine Ari, stop worrying.'

Silence, because they both knew she was not as fine as her family would like her to be.

'I'll be home in a few hours.'

More silence and sighs from the other end as Ari searched for the right words. Silence happened a lot. People too fearful of saying the wrong thing generally opted to say nothing at all.

'Oh, and can you let mum know I'm coming home please? Thanks sis. I love you.'

She turned the tap on and looked around the kitchen, willing away the memories that lingered around her like shadows. Carter grabbing her by the waist and spinning her around. Kisses peppering her neck as she tried to shrug him off half-heartedly. Laughter. So much laughter. She had ribbed him end-lessly about having a surname as a first name and he would always bring up his nickname from school, which had been Carter the farter. They used to col-lapse in fits of laughter. And then there was the dark-ness. A darkness that filled her from the inside out and stole her soul, and her marriage. Grief did that to you.

Mel grabbed her keys and stepped outside where she breathed in the woody scent of flora and fauna. She walked towards the car and away from the house, stopping momentarily to breathe in the sweet earthy smell of the shady old oak tree. As a child she'd been fascinated by the colour changing lichen that grew on the trunk. It would turn from brown to green when wet and she had been convinced the tree was magic.

She drove over the tree's gnarly roots that snaked in and out of the earth. The house was a shrinking image in her mirror as she made her way from Coniston back towards her hometown of Dunbar. Ahead of her she had a three-hour drive and plenty of time to prepare herself for a lecture from her mum and sister.

The rolling hills distracted her for a while, greens of different shades fighting against the browns and reds of moss and shrubs free to spread wherever they wanted. This was what she had first loved about the area when she'd visited as a child with her parents. There had been something comforting about being on a road with hills either side throwing their different shades of light across the landscape, and the older she got the more her soul craved it. Dunbar was a windy, cold harbour town, and although there were hills and scenery within driving distance, Mel still preferred the stillness and beauty of the Lake District.

Mel felt her stomach sink as her mum's house came into view. Living with her mum had been a blessing after Ella had died, but her mum had become over-protective, and it felt as if every move Mel made was under scrutiny. As she pulled onto the drive her sister was standing at the door, arms folded in a way that did little to quell her anxiety.

'I know, I know.' Mel exited the car with her hands up in surrender. 'I know that you hate me right now for worrying you, but I had to get away.'

Birds screamed in the air above and Mel felt like joining them.

'That's the thing Mel, you keep running and I'm wondering when you're going to stop and allow yourself to heal,' Ari said.

Mel could feel rage rise within her like a phoenix. 'Allow myself to heal. *Allow* myself to heal? You have no idea how it feels to lose a child, Ari.'

Grace appeared in the doorway, glancing between her two daughters and then gingerly towards the neighbouring houses.

Ari opened her mouth as if she intended to speak but thought better of it.

Tears replaced anger as they rolled down Mel's face. Her mum and sister whispered something to each other.

'That's right, you and Mum discuss me like a project.' Mel stood against her car, contemplating her next move, aware that she had not attempted to enter the house. The very thought of them following her around grilling her made her stomach churn. She hated that she reacted, but she was over being watched like a child. And how was she meant to heal? That was to date the stupidest comment to fall out of her sister's mouth.

She drove away with pleas from her mum and Ari echoing behind her through the open window. Her mind was a whirl of conflicting thoughts and emotions: guilt mixed with a good dose of sadness and anger. So much anger at her sister for telling her to heal. She passed by the grey houses and people scurrying in and out of shops like an army of ants and she kept driving, eager to put distance between herself and her family. The cliffs along the coastal route teased at the ocean that lay beyond them as wind whipped the long grass back and forth like a metronome. It felt soothing.

She arrived at The Crab & Claw pub, turned the ignition off and closed her eyes, trying to block out the image of her mum crying.

'Fuck it,' she said out loud as she stepped out of the car, still troubled by her sister's words. She had intended to go for a walk along the beach, but her legs were carrying her into the bar and her mouth was ordering a drink. She sat outside where she could look at the sea and listen to the waves crashing against the rocks. The smell of the ocean's breath permeated the atmosphere around her, reminding her of happy childhood times.

'It's a lovely view, isn't it?' Mel turned her to her right and there was a man who she'd guess to be in his sixties, sitting by himself with a pint.

'It is a nice view, but it's a bit cool out here with that wind.'

He nodded and turned to look into the distance. She studied his face and hands weathered like the rocks and felt a surge of sadness for him sitting there alone. She stood and moved to join him, welcoming the distraction from her thoughts.

'You don't mind me sitting here, do you?' Mel asked the stranger as she approached him.

'Not at all love, I'm glad of the company.' He smiled, revealing a row of worn dentures.

'Do you live here or are you visiting?'

'I live over there in one of those bungalows.' He pointed towards a row of four petite cottages that all looked identical with their red doors and white net curtain windows. 'We moved in two years ago when my wife couldn't manage the stairs anymore. She died just over a year ago.' His eyes held a sadness that his voice did not relay.

'Oh. I'm sorry to hear that. It must be lonely for you living by yourself.' Her heart misfired for a second or two and Mel felt the ground beneath her shift.

'Some days it is lonely, other days I don't notice it so much. I talk to her all the time. Only in the house, mind you, otherwise people will think I'm crackers.' He laughed.

'Tell me about yourself,' Mel said. 'You must have so many stories and I'd love to hear a few of them.'

'Well young lady, in my seventy-six years on earth I don't think anyone under the age of fifty has ever asked me to talk about myself. Come to think of it, not many over fifty have asked me either.' He smiled but continued. 'Okay I will, but on one condition.'

'What's that?' Mel asked.

'You let me buy you a drink and some food.'

Mel screwed her face up. 'Can I pass on the food? I ate not long ago, but I will have a pint.'

The stranger chuckled to himself and muttered something about young people today as he walked back into the pub.

Mel watched a seagull fight against the wind overhead, its cries blown away. She wondered what it would be like to step off the cliff into the blue water below and she walked towards the edge, as if pulled by an invisible string. She looked down into the ocean and held on to the handrail as she watched waves crash off jagged rocks and foam spray into the air like paint splattered onto an easel.

Would she regret it if she stepped off? Would she claw her way through the air trying to stop the descent, or would she fall arms wide, welcoming the end? She imagined sinking into the briny depths below, a human mermaid until life ebbed away. She filled her lungs, trying to imagine what the sensation of drowning would feel like, but she soon exhaled, desperate for breath.

'Watch that wind doesn't send you flying over the edge, there's not a lot of you.' Mel turned and smiled at her new friend as he placed drinks on the table. She walked back towards him and sat down on the wooden seat, noting the surface of the table that was worn with both the wind and the sea air. 'I'm Joe by the way. I thought I should introduce myself seeing as I'm about to share a story with you.'

'Thanks Joe, next round is on me.'

'Relax lass, have your drink while I answer the question you asked me. But first you can tell me your name, so I don't have to keep calling you lass.'

'My name is Melody, but I prefer Mel, it's way cooler. No one is called Melody! My sis is called Aria, but we call her Ari. My dad was a music teacher, in case you hadn't guessed. Lucky us, aye?'

Joe looked thoughtful before speaking. 'It could be worse. I went to school with a girl called Mildred.'

They both laughed and Mel agreed that Mildred was worse than Melody, but only just.

'So, what story would you like to share with me, Joe?'

'Why are you so interested in my story? A young woman like you should be interested in people her own age. Speaking of which, why aren't you with your friends or boyfriend? Why are you hanging out with an old guy like me? Not that I'm complaining, mind you.'

Mel waved her arm, dismissing what he'd said. 'Let's just say something happened to me, and it's made me realise we walk through life asking people how they are but not *really* asking how they are. We don't listen to what people say because we're so busy, maybe self absorbed to a degree. Most of us are caught in the trap of working to buy more, people seem less happy, and we're more disconnected than ever. It's sad.'

Joe pulled his mouth down, Robert De Niro style. 'That's deep for someone so young. As for a story, let me think.' His fore finger and thumb caressed his stubbled chin as he looked into his beer. 'Would you rather hear *Monkey Business* or *Bomb Shell*?'

'Mm, both sound intriguing but I think we will go with *Bomb Shell*.'

Joe shuffled himself to face Mel and then looked over her shoulder, gathering his memories.

'I was four years old and living in Aberdeen. The date was the twenty-first of April nineteen forty-three, and the day started as normal. Every morning I would get out of bed and sit at the kitchen table waiting for my breakfast, which was usually porridge. Some mornings I would take the ashes out from the fire and if the wind was blowing the wrong way it would blow as much back onto me as went in the bin. I had a younger sister, Ada, she was what Mam called a grizzly baby, so Mam spent a lot of time fussing about her. I was allowed outside to play, not that we had a lot to play with back in those days, a ball usually, but I would kick about the street with the other boys. I was young but the older kids knew to look after us, and back then you did as your parents said. There was no back chat or cheek because it would have been slapped out of you.' Joe took a swig from his pint and swallowed half of it. 'I'm not boring you, am I?'

'No, not at all, please, keep going.'

'Early evening, we ate dinner, which was a meat-free stew with bread, no butter as that was a rarity, but we would spread the bread with a bit of dripping. Anyway, as I said, I ate, and then had a bath in the kitchen. We didn't have a bathroom back then, so I had my bath in a tin tub that was placed in front of the fire in the kitchen. Mam would boil the kettle and fill pans with water to warm the metal up, but the water never stayed warm for long. My dad worked at the local coal mine, and he would come home with black dust ingrained on his hands. My mam would top up the bath and dad would scrub as much of the coal dust off him as possible. We were still at war with the Germans, World War II, and as dusk fell each night, we would block out all light from inside. Blackout curtains were hung at windows and draught excluders made up of old newspapers stuffed inside of material were placed in front of doors. Candles gave us enough light to get around the house, and we weren't allowed to open the door to go outside to the toilet, so we used bedpans at night.

'This night started as any other except this night, the twenty-first of April, would be the night bombs dropped on Aberdeen. I was in my bed when the sirens started screaming. My parents grabbed my sister who was sleeping in her cot, and we all squashed into a small cupboard in their bedroom with pillows up against the door to rest our heads on. Ada screamed with confusion and fought against being held still. It was so dark in that cupboard, and I can still remember my heart beating as wildly as a galloping stallion. The sirens continued to scream and then bangs, the loudest bangs I had ever heard, followed by lots of shaking. Everything around us felt as if it shifted. Mam was crying and the air in the cupboard seemed to shrink with every passing second and I felt as if I was breathing through a straw. I have no idea how long we were in there, but it felt like it was days, not hours, and when we left it was almost daylight.

'I remember my parents checking the house over before me and Ada were allowed out of the bedroom. Mam's voice was shaking when she came back in, saying that at least our house was still standing. I'm still not sure I knew what had happened at that stage. At least not until I was allowed outside, and I remember stepping outside as if it were yesterday.' Joe shook his head and his eyes misted over, moist with memories.

'The first thing I noticed was that the air was thick with dust that followed you wherever you went. The street that our row of houses looked on to was flat to the ground at one end, and there were men pulling bricks and mortar from piles of rubble and women wailing as they held tightly to their children. Some of my friends were killed that night and at four years old I struggled to understand I would never see them again. I got no comfort from being told they were in heaven. To me it was just a word, and although I was too young to understand the concept of death, I developed an intense fear of my parents disappearing. All in all, ninety-eight civilians lost their lives that night.'

'I can't even imagine how awful that must have been and how terrified you must have felt,' Mel said.

Joe shook his head as if trying to shake off memories. 'As the sun set that night, I remember a fear settling within me that felt bigger than me. I was terrified to close my eyes. The dark never bothered me until the night of the Blitz. Now it held so much, it immobilised me. I would tremble in my bed and cry, begging Mam to let me lie in the bed with her and Dad. Nothing seemed the same after that. People were quiet, footy games weren't the same without our goalkeeper William. Sid, who used to ruffle the top of my head if I scored. And John, the only one of us who had been able to do tricks with the ball. It was never the same again. We played footy amongst the dust and rubble, but we didn't have the same innocence that we'd had previously. It really was life changing for all of us kids, and of course the parents. It's almost as if it left a hole in you that could never be filled. Even to this day when I think back to it, my body remembers. My heart races and I swear I can smell dust in the air, thick as treacle.'

Mel thought about his words and struggled to find words for such a harrowing tale. 'I'm so sorry you experienced that, Joe. I can't even imagine how terrifying it must have been.'

'Occasionally I still have nightmares, but I've reached a good age, which is more than my friends did that night,' He said sombrely. 'And seeing as I have shared a bit about myself with you, I would love to know what your story is Mel.'

Feeling uninhibited after the alcohol, Mel nodded. 'I'll summarize, it makes it easier to say and believe me when I say, you don't want me to start crying.' She took a deep breath and prepared herself. 'Well, as I said earlier, I have one sister. My dad died when I was fifteen and I still miss him every day. My mum, Grace, never remarried or even dated anyone for that matter, I think she's too busy worrying about me.'

'Why would she be worrying about you?'

'Life went tits up Joe. Five years ago, I married my soul mate, and we built our own house in the Lake District. It was a big thing for me leaving my mum and sister, but my husband Carter was offered a job in Keswick, and we decided to embrace the curve ball rather than run from it. Life was peachy. We had a baby, a girl named Ella and,' Mel swallowed down the emotion that threatened to spill out of her. 'When she was three years old, she died.' Mel picked up her drink and drained the glass, avoiding eye contact with Joe.

'Oh love, I am sor-.'

'Just popping to the toilet and I'll get us another drink.' She said quickly, her legs carrying her away from the heaviness of that conversation and the threat of a meltdown.

They continued drinking and talking for a while longer until the sun set, and the sky turned a velvety darkness that was starting to reflect Mel's mood.

Joe staggered home, leaving Mel by herself to pick through the thoughts of her fuddled mind. She was drunk by then and she wanted to apologize to her mum and sister for worrying them. She remembered she had her car with her. A taxi home would cost a fortune. Home. She'd not checked her phone for hours and her anger had dissipated since hearing Joe's story. Now she just felt a heavy sadness hanging over her, seeping into her bones along with the cold night air. Her phone was not in her bag, so she checked under the table and couldn't find it.

She walked into the bar and propped herself against it, unsteady on her feet. She felt sleepy and he head lolled to the side as if too heavy to support itself. 'Excuse me, has a phone been handed in?'

The barman shook his head. 'We won't be able to serve you any more drinks either, miss. You've had enough.'

'I only want my phone!' she said, the words coiling slowly out of her mouth. People were looking at her, so she walked toward the door and accidentally pulled over a chair that her bag had managed to hook itself around. Before she picked the chair up a guy in a black suit and white shirt appeared out of nowhere.

'Do we have a problem?' he looked from the bar staff to Mel, and back again.

Mel was now aware she had become the focal point in the room.

'Just leaving.' Her words slurred as she stumbled past him and made her way outside. The wind whipped her hair around her face, making it hard to see where her car was parked. To her left she could hear the angry roar of the ocean, but she steered clear of the cliff edge and lurched around until she found her car. It took her several attempts to find the keys in her bag before she finally opened the car door and manoeuvred herself into the driver's seat. She let out a sigh and just as she was about to turn the key in the ignition, the doorman from the pub opened the car door and grabbed the keys out of the ignition.

'There's no way I can let you drive off. You need a taxi.'

'I'm sleeping. I mean, going to sleep in the car.' Mel said, the words stumbling from her mouth as if too lazy to form properly.

'Don't you have a home to go to?' the man asked.

'Too far.' she waved her hand dismissively too tired to talk. 'Dunbar.' She added slowly. He rubbed his head in irritation, then walked towards the pub. Mel closed the door and realised he still had her keys, but she was too drunk to follow him.

Mel woke briefly sometime later when the car door opened, but she was disoriented and sleepy, so sleepy that she went along with the voice guiding her into another car.

Mel opened her eyes. Holy fuck, what was wrong with her head? The pounding was intense. She looked at the sofa and took in the room. She had never seen them before. Bile scorched the back of her throat as she tried to recall the previous evening, but she drew a blank beyond drinking with Joe.

'Oh, you're awake,' a male voice said, and she froze. She looked up and a man she had never seen before stood in the doorway. He had a bald head, was wearing jeans and a tight t-shirt, his arms and neck were covered in tattoos, and he looked as if his favourite sport might be MMA. A smell of bacon lingered behind him, and it made her want to vomit. She never could face food after a big night of drinking.

'Who are you?' Mel's heart knocked an unsteady rhythm in her chest.

'You don't remember?' He had a quizzical look on his face, trying to hold a laugh in.

'No, I don't, and I want to leave please.' Thankfully her clothes were still on, and her bag lay on the floor next to the sofa so clearly nothing had happened.

'It's okay. You can leave, Mel. I'm not holding you hostage. In fact, I pretty much saved your arse last night. I'm Carl. I work in the Crab & Claw.' He paused. 'The doorman?' He raised his eyebrows, waiting for the penny to drop. 'You were pretty messed up last night.'

'Tell me about it, my head's about to explode. I have no memory of anything much after the old man called Joe left.'

'You can't keep up with the likes of Joe when it comes to pints. He's had way too much practice over the years compared to you.'

Mel braced herself. 'Dare I ask what I did?'

'You didn't really do anything. It was more what you were going to do. The bar stopped serving you, but you left without too much fuss. I watched you because I've not seen you around here before, and I don't mean that in a creepy way either. You got in your car and there was no way I could let you drive, so I took the keys off you. When I came back you were fast asleep, so I left you there until the end of my shift and brought you here to sleep it off. And before you ask, I was a perfect gentleman.'

'Thank you and sorry, I'm more than a little embarrassed. But while I'm here, could I ask for some water and paracetamol please?' Heat flooded her face.

He snorted a laugh and walked into another room. 'You need to look after yourself a little better because not everyone is as trustworthy as me, so next time leave your car at home,' he said, as he handed her the water, a box of paracetamol and her phone. 'It was under the table you were sat at. It is your phone, right?'

Mel sat in her car as shame washed over her. Twice this week she'd been missing in action. At least last time she had been safe in her own house, but this, this was just embarrassing. Thankfully it wasn't on her doorstep because she'd never be able to look that man in the eye again, or go back to that pub.

Driving home from the Crab & Claw, Mel was thinking about Joe and his story about the war, when a police car got her attention, siren blaring. She slowed, waiting for it to pass but it pulled up behind her and the policeman indicated for her to pull over. Her heart rate, which was already ramped up due to last night's alcohol, picked up pace as the officer walked towards her car.

'Can I have your license, please?' the policeman said, as he pulled a notebook from his pocket.

'I, erm, I don't have it with me sorry,' Mel replied.

'Can you tell me your full name and date of birth please?' he asked, before jotting down the information Mel gave him.

He walked a few steps away from her car while speaking on his radio. Mel tried to steady her shaking hands and calm her breathing as she watched him walk back to her car. 'Ma'am, you were reported as a missing person yesterday.'

Mel flushed red. 'Oh. Right. My family are a bit OTT when it comes to answering calls but as you can see, I am fine and I'm actually on my way home now.'

'Normally I would do an assessment to check your wellbeing and encourage you to return home, but I can smell alcohol on your breath. Have you been drinking?' the officer asked.

This could not be happening. Mel watched as the officer unwrapped a nozzle and placed it into a machine.

'Breathe into this tube until I tell you to stop. Keep going, keep going—'

The machines beeped and Mel felt as if time stood still.

'I'm sorry to say you are over the legal limit of twenty-two micrograms of alcohol per one hundred ml of breath and have failed your test. You will be required to take two further tests once we are at the station.'

The officer instructed her to get into the back of the police car. She was in a real police car for committing an actual offence. She was the woman who returned ten pence to the shop once when she was overpaid.

At the police station she was issued with a fine of five hundred pounds and a driving ban for twelve months. Thoughts bounced around her head. How would she get to work? How would she make a living?

Eventually she was ushered out of the police station by her red-eyed mum, like some sort of fragile child. Her mum wrapped a blanket around her shoulders as if trying to hide her from the world, but she was too numb and exhausted to care.

Six weeks later

The feeling of darkness continued to grow within her like a rotten weed, blocking out light. It made everything feel so much harder, like a chainmail overcoat. Sometimes Mel was so exhausted that even forming words and pushing them out of her mouth was too much effort. She tried, she really did, but no one seemed to understand the weight of the darkness she carried around with her. Sleep was bittersweet. She welcomed the escape from faces, voices, and talking. So much talking.

CHAPTER 2

—·—

MEL

Mel walked into the restaurant to find Jade and Emma already seated. Jade had called her almost daily, and Mel knew that she had hurt her friend of twenty-two years by ignoring some of her calls. but she felt as if her life had spiralled out of control, and she had no words to explain this to others. It was seven weeks since she'd lost her driving licence and nausea clawed at her throat as she painted a fake smile on her face. Her friends made anxious eye contact with each other before waving frantically and hugging her too tightly.

'Hi babe, did your mum drop you off?' Jade asked.

'Yes,' said Mel. 'But I won't be drinking,' she added a little too quickly. 'I hope you don't mind.'

'Of course not,' they both chimed in unison, but there was a stiffness about them that told her that this was hard for them. 'How is your mum? I've not seen her for ages?' Emma was acting weird, making Mel feel edgy.

'She's fine, busy with her voluntary work which keeps her occupied two days a week.'

'And Ari. Is she okay?' Jade asked.

Mel felt as if she was in an interview, and paranoid that one of them would bring up the drink driving charge. 'Ari's fine. Shall we order dinner?' They ordered food and the conversation ranged from new washing machines to holidays and recipes. Mel noticed that neither of them asked her how she was. Her chest felt tight, the conversation forced to the point that she felt as if they were all acting. She looked at her friends, whom she had known most of her life and wondered if she really knew them at all. They obviously wanted her to leave. They kept looking at each other and she was certain they talked about her when they went to the bar.

She heard someone laughing and looked across the room. A tall man was looking at her, mouth open, laughing at her brazenly. She wondered if she had food on her face, or maybe she just had the kind of face people laugh at.

Someone had turned up the volume in the room and the noise became all-consuming. People were talking way too loudly. Laughter, too much laughter, and she couldn't help but feel it was directed at her.

She stood and pushed her chair back. 'I have to go,' she said, before making a quick escape. She could hear her friends calling after her but neither followed her. She felt a mixture of relief and disappointment.

Outside she pulled her coat tightly around herself to keep out the cold already penetrating through to her bones. She ordered a taxi and breathed a sigh of relief when it arrived. She allowed the tears to rush down her cheeks, anger and confusion swimming around her head.

Why would her friends talk about her? Why would people that she didn't even know laugh at her? It made her wonder what rumours had been circulating, and she knew it would be a long time before she stepped back into a restaurant or bar.

The house smelled of pine disinfectant and furniture polish as Mel stepped through the front door. She wished there was a secret tunnel that would take her to her room and bypass the conversations she would be forced to have with her mum.

'You're early.' Her mum looked up from the book she was reading, No Mud, No Lotus. Mel got the concept that without pain or suffering there can be no happiness, but surely her mum did not think this analogy applied to her situation. 'What's happened?' she asked, using the same tone she used to use when Mel was younger. It implied she was guilty, even when she wasn't.

'Nothing happened. I'm fine.' Mel rushed upstairs and shut the door behind her, standing against it in the hope that her mum would not follow and shout her concerns through the door. It felt like she was a teenager again, avoiding her mother because everything about her drove her crazy; only this time around she thought it might be mutual.

She slept until noon the following day and when she woke, she felt as if she had been on a two-day bender. Her body was stiff and achy, her head thumping. She thought back to last night: she had no alcohol, so why did she feel so crap? She walked downstairs to get a drink of water and her mum lowered her glasses as if to get a better look at her. The dining room table was strewn with card, craft materials and a glue gun and some half-completed Christmas cards, most likely for one of her mum's fund-raising events.

'You're not dressed.'

Mel really hated when her mother made such obvious statements. She said nothing because she had no energy to engage in conversation with her.

'Mel.' Her mum followed her into the kitchen, standing behind her like a shadow.

'Yes?'

'Are you okay?'

Many replies scrolled through Mel's head, none of them suitable to be verbalised. 'I'm fine Mum, I'm tired. Maybe I'm getting the flu, I'm just going to sleep it off.'

'I thought you weren't drinking last night?'

She closed her eyes and willed herself not to bite. 'Bad choice of words, I meant sleep off whatever it is I'm feeling. And no, it's not a hangover. Do we have paracetamol?' The house phone rang, and her mum rushed to answer it.

'Grace speaking.' She said before wandering off into another room. Mel quickly swallowed the tablets she'd found in the first aid box while her mum was talking, and then she climbed the stairs with heavy legs, and she crawled back into bed.

Mel woke drenched in sweat. Whispers of memories hung in the air, then disintegrated. Her mind felt heavy with things she couldn't make sense of, her body felt weighed down making it uncomfortable to move in bed. She had no idea what day it was or when she last ate anything.

There was a knock on her door and then Ari popped her head into the room. 'Hey sis, fancy a visitor?'

'If you want, but I don't feel well, so...' She hoped the unspoken words would encourage Ari out the door. They didn't.

Her sister looked around the room and wrinkled her nose. 'I could let some air in here if you like?' Without waiting for a reply, she leaned towards the window and opened it. It was annoying.

Mel tutted.

Ari turned away from the window. 'Do you want me to close it?'

'Whatever.'

'Mel, talk to me.' There was a pleading in her voice that irritated. 'Mum told me that you went out the other night with some friends and when you came home, she said you weren't yourself. She could tell you had been crying. Please, tell me what happened? We want to help but you keep shutting us out.'

Mel swallowed back a wave of tears and tried to form a sentence, but her brain had scrambled everything, and she had no idea what to say or where to start. She avoided looking at Ari and all she could do was shake her head. She could feel worry radiating off her sister in waves and it added to her feeling of despair. She was causing stress to the people she loved. A tear rolled down her face.

'Oh, Mel,' Ari hugged her, and Mel broke. She cried like a baby, and it felt good to let it out, but she knew it was temporary and before long the darkness would settle back over her like a cloak.

'Is there anything I can do?' Ari asked. 'I hate to even ask this in case it upsets you, but would it help to talk to Carter? Maybe he will understand.' Ari stiffened in anticipation of a response.

'I don't know what I need, but I do know it's not Carter.' she said flatly, 'and asking me just adds to how I feel.'

'Sorry.' A pause. 'You understand Mum and I have to ask, though? You know we want to help because we love you?'

She nodded but deep inside couldn't help feeling she was nothing more than a burden.

'How about we have a weekend in York?' Ari asked brightly. 'We could book a spa and go shopping, eat some nice food?'

Ari's face was lit up and it felt wrong to say no, but Mel had no desire to leave her bedroom. 'Please, Mel. For me. Think how happy it will make Mum.'

'It's September and it's freezing. It won't be any fun walking around in the cold,' Mel replied.

'We'll be inside more than out, and we live in Scotland in case you've forgotten. Just wrap up and you'll be fine.'

Mel stared out of the train window. Houses flashed past as she listened to Ari tell her all about her boyfriend Jay's family. She nodded politely, raised her eyebrows where appropriate and threw in the occasional "Mmhmm" to appease her. She'd been pressured into going to York by her mum, who'd fretted around her after she'd said she didn't feel up to it. Now, as she listened to her sister chunter on, she wished she'd come alone. At least she would've been able to lie in bed all day without people bothering her. Anxiety swelled inside her, so she pulled out a can of vodka, lime, and soda from her bag.

'Want one?' she asked her sister as she handed a can toward her.

'It's a little early, isn't it?'

'Stop being such an old woman and just have one.' Mel handed her a can and turned towards the window. The clouds rolled past as if on fast forward and the sky was bleak and threatening, but as she sipped the vodka it relaxed her almost instantly. She passed another drink to her sister as soon as she had finished hers.

Ari took it reluctantly. 'I'm not having any more after this Mel, I want to go shopping and I thought we could do some sight-seeing, or maybe we could go to the flicks and watch a movie?'

'Maybe tomorrow, Ari. Today I just want to chill.'

'Does chill mean drink yourself into oblivion?'

Her discomfort was palpable, and Mel laughed loudly.

Ari flushed and looked around the train carriage self consciously. 'Can you tone it down?'

'Sorry sis. You're so uptight, though. Just relax, will you? A few drinks won't hurt us.'

A few hours later, they sat in a restaurant overlooking the river. Heaters warmed the room to a toasty temperature while a man played the piano in the background. Mel reflected on her last experience of being in a bar restaurant and it reminded her that Emma had only contacted her once since that day. This environment, however, felt relaxed, and she felt better than she had in months.

'Mel, stop shouting, people are looking,' Ari whispered as she looked around the room, cheeks flushed.

'I'm not shouting, You sound like Mum. What you need is a few more drinks and then you might relax and not care about all of these strangers in the room.' Mel could feel the knot in her stomach unravel with each sip of alcohol and it felt good.

'You're drunk. You always shout when you're drunk, it's so embarrassing! When did you last eat something? Actually, don't answer that. I'm ordering some food for us.'

'Sis, I'm old enough to know when I want to eat, ta very much. You order food for you but I'm getting some cocktails for us. Lighten up, we're on holiday and you wanted me to be happy didn't you?'

Her head pulsed like a beating heart, each pump ripping through her, intensifying as she moved. She needed water. She winced as she entered the bathroom and light hit her eyes. What happened? Flashes came at her: drinking on the train, shopping, the restaurant, and the huge fishbowl cocktails. She looked to where Ari should be sleeping, and the bed was empty. She checked her phone, and it was one pm. Holy shit!

She sent a text. *I just woke up sis, sorry! What happened lol? How's your head? Mine is banging!! X*

Mel looked at herself in the mirror. Impressive eye bags and dark circles made her look like a cross between an addict and someone who didn't care about their appearance. She glugged water while throwing back two tablets for her head and she had a nauseating flashback of the time she woke up in that strange bouncer man's house after she been to the Crab & Claw.

Her phone pinged. *Welcome to the land of the living! Where to start with last night?? You got so drunk and started playing the piano, only we both know you don't play the piano, so it was kind of awkward. You knocked a table of drinks over and flipped at a guy who asked you to leave, and then you started crying and wouldn't stop. You were passed out by seven pm. Honestly, I was mortified Mel.*

She could taste the bitterness of her shame and wished more than anything that she'd stayed at home curled up in her bed with her mum checking in on her. She had been having such a good time and now it was same old routine with her making a show of herself.

Mel stood under the shower, inhaling the lemongrass and ginger scent of the free bodywash. It smelled like Thailand, and she wished she could fuck off and live there all alone. Her head shook from the inside out and her guts were riding a storm. She dried herself quickly and packed her bag before her sister got back. The embarrassment was too much, and Ari would already have called Mum and told her. She couldn't face another concerned lecture. She sent a text to Ari: *I had to leave. Sorry.*

Her phone rang at the train station, and she chose to ignore it as she stepped onboard and took a seat. The swaying carriage and repetitive clicking of the train on the tracks was soothing. She closed her eyes, wishing away the previous day.

CHAPTER 3

— • —

GRACE

Grace had always loved the theatre, ever since she was a child, and at sixty-one, her love for all things theatrical had only grown. She waved to her friend Karen, who had just walked through the restaurant doors. It was Karen's birthday, and they were going to the theatre after a meal at their favourite restaurant. Grace answered her phone that had rang for the third time since she'd sat down.

'Hi Ari, I'm just out to lunch with Karen are you and Mel having a nice time?' Grace asked.

'Things haven't exactly gone as I'd expected Mum.'

'What do you mean? That sounds rather ominous.'

'Well, Mel started drinking on the train, which is no big deal, but by the time we got to York she was a bit drunk. After shopping we went for food, and she kept drinking. She barely ate and next thing she's falling over someone's table, and then things just got worse from there. She even bulldozed the piano player out of the way and made a total show of herself trying to play it.'

'The piano! My God, you couldn't get her near a musical instrument as a child, not for want of trying either on your father's part. What on Earth did she think she was doing? And is she okay?'

'That's the thing. She's gone.'

'Gone where? Shopping? Drinking?' Grace asked.

'I left her sleeping this morning, I figured she must need it and I met up with a few friends who are here for the weekend. She messaged me just after lunch and asked what had happened last night. I told her and then twenty minutes later she sent a text saying *"Sorry, I have to leave."*

'Have you checked the room?' Grace mouthed the word 'sorry' to Karen.

'Yes, and she's gone, and her phone is switched off,' Ari said. 'Sorry Mum, I don't want to spoil your weekend, but you need to know because she will be on her way back home now.'

'Okay. Maybe this is our fault for pressuring her. Are you staying or coming home?' Grace asked.

'I'm staying, but I'll be home tomorrow.'

Grace ended the call and a feeling of unease settle inside of her. She stood to hug Karen.

'Is everything okay?' Karen asked, her brow furrowed in concern.

'I'm sorry, I hate taking calls when I'm in a restaurant. It's so rude and I usually would ignore it but when there were 3 missed calls, I knew Aria needed to speak to me. Mel's not doing too good. They're in York and Mel has left while Aria was out with some friends. She's on her way home. Whoever said kids get easier as they get older was a liar.' She was trying to make light of it, but Grace knew truth coated each word.

'We can cancel the show if you like?' Karen smiled.

'No, I won't hear of it, it's your birthday. I'll call Mel when we've eaten but we'll still go, besides, I've been looking forward to it for weeks.' She looked at Karen, her dear friend. They met each other in the doctor's surgery when they were both pregnant and attending antenatal appointments. She had been pregnant with Aria, Karen with her only child Karl, now twenty-eight and a dentist. Karen was still happily married to Tim and sometimes Grace envied her. Not in a bad way, just in a missing her own man kind of way.

Tom had always been Grace's voice of reason when her worries took over and now with all of this worry about Mel, she missed him more than ever. Life could be terribly cruel sometimes and Grace had been dealt a tough hand when Tom died of a heart attack almost ten years ago. She had been thankful that the girls were still young enough to need looking after because without them she may well have given up,

Grace was pleased that Karen sat next to an inquisitive child in the theatre who asked more questions than her friend could answer, because her mind was working overtime. She had called Mel, who had not answered. Now she was imagining all kinds of potential reasons why, and all of them had a negative outcome. Trying to stay calm and not catastrophise felt like a huge effort, because part of her brain seemed to function best in the 'what ifs.' No one ever warned you as an expectant mum or young parent that one day you might have to watch your adult child self-de-struct.

She glanced around the theatre hall and wondered what secrets and challenges the people might be dealing with. She time-travelled backwards to when the girls were young. It was Mel's first trip to the theatre for her fourth birthday to see *Chitty Chitty Bang Bang.* Little Mel had been mesmerised by the flying car and by the character *Truly Scrumptious,* so impressed by the show she declared very sincerely that she was going to be an actress when she grew up. Now as Grace sat in the same theatre, it felt empty despite being full of people and noise. Kookaburra laughter pierced the air as people applauded the actors for their comedy inserts, but she felt no joy. She was relieved when it ended, and she could leave.

She knew as soon as she opened the door that Mel was not in the house because it was in complete darkness, but she still yelled up the stairs and checked her room. She phoned her again and it went straight to voicemail. A sickly feeling settled in her stomach, and she wished more than anything that she had someone else to heap some of this onto. She switched on the TV and started knitting to try and distract herself while she glanced at her phone, willing it to ring.

CHAPTER 4

MEL

Mel wrapped the blanket tightly around her body and squeezed her eyes shut in the hope that the nurse would leave her alone, but Helen was still there standing next to her bed like an unwanted visitor. Helen was a jovial woman only a few years older than Mel, but for some reason she seemed decades older. She was very calm, kind, and patient, and she had a quietness about her that belied the mental strength she must have to work in such a place as this.

Mel had agreed to go into the wellbeing centre after she had failed to return home from York. She'd not been able to face her family, so she had travelled to London with no real idea of what she would do when she got there. This resulted in her losing her job, which in itself was no big deal because it was a casual position and not a job she was passionate about. Before Ella had died Mel had worked as a PA to a well-respected law firm, and yet here she was without any work at all now, and when you are already weighed down by shame, guilt, and despair, you just don't have the mental strength to face your fuck ups. She had felt sure that she was doing her family a favour staying out of their way, unable to contemplate the worry they would go through, but she ran out of money and had called her oldest friend, Jade. Jade agreed to catch the train to London with a promise of giving Mel some money. It turned out to be a false promise. When Jade stepped off the train, Ari followed her, and Mel was too exhausted and defeated to do anything other than return home. She had been shocked to see how much weight her mum had lost and when her sister suggested Mel seek professional help, she felt obliged to agree. She was lost and she had no idea to find her way out of the darkness. She was also aware that her life was spiralling out of control as she blindly stepped into the world of allowing other people to decide what was best for her.

'Come on Mel, just take your meds and you will get a good night's sleep,' the nurse said.

'I don't want to.' She was aware that she sounded like a petulant child. 'Sleep! What's that, anyway? All I know is those pills make me feel as if bugs are crawling inside my skin. You try sleeping with that happening.'

'Well, you need to speak to Dr Thomas about that, honey. I'm just under orders to make sure you take them.'

'So, you're basically the thief of my human rights? You take my right to say no away from me?'

The nurse looked surprised.

'I'm not getting into that with you, Mel. Just take the tablets, please?'

Mel relented and swallowed the medication. It was another day, same routine.

The nurse left the room and came straight back in. 'Mel, I forgot to pass on a message from earlier. A man called Carter rang and asked for details about visiting hours. I told him that he would only be allowed to visit with your permission.' She waited in doorway longer than she needed to.

'Thanks. He won't be coming in.' Mel said, wondering how he knew. If he'd found out through anyone other than her family that meant her being here was common knowledge. And if her family had told Carter, well, she would have something to say about that.

The following morning, she woke with sweat pouring out of her, breath ragged with adrenalin after another night fuelled by drug induced sleep. Memories spun around her like a merry-go-round; too fast to get a glimpse of before they're gone again. Her head was swimming, and her eyes felt as if they were weighed down. She trudged out of bed only because she needed to use the bathroom. Showering felt like a mission, but she had to attend the group therapy today and meet with Dr Thomas, who had already made it clear if she did not start engaging, she wouldn't be going home anytime soon. She had been here for five weeks, and every day felt the same. Never ending noise, nurses, pills, doctors, meetings, group activities. Repeat, repeat, repeat.

Time slid effortlessly between past and present like a ski on snow. She was unsure what was real as everything merged and separated. Holding on to any one thought felt impossible. She saw faces, mouths moving as words came out, but it was as if there was something between her and the rest of the world, an invisible shield that kept her separate. Nothing excited her, food tasted bland, and she struggled to find joy in anything. The worst part was seeing the looks upon the faces of the people who loved her.

'It's Tuesday Mel, time for your appointment.'

She looked at Nurse Tess, one of the nice ones, and wondered if she is married. She pictured Tess at home with a big dog lying on the floor beside her chair and a large glass of wine to help her relax after the stressful day at work. She also wondered why anyone would want this job.

'Come on love, you don't want to be late for Dr. Thomas,' Tess said.

Mel forced her feet to move and examined her socks while shuffling along the floor like a penguin. She wondered why her mother thought it was appropriate to buy her socks with cats on. She fucking hated cats.

She sat on the white plastic chair, cold to the touch. The reception desk was enclosed on both sides with a partial open front counter. The young blonde woman who was usually there had been replaced by a woman with dark hair. The room was silent except for the click of the keyboard in the background. An air purifier pumped out clouds of lemon scented smoke into the air like an industrial chimney, and a picture of a beach hung slightly crooked on the wall. The clock slowed in places like this.

There were six chairs in total, but Mel had only ever seen two of them filled at once. She flicked through a magazine until the doctor made an appearance. She still felt angry about the socks she was wearing.

Today the doctor was dressed in all beige which summed up his personality: boring. His room smelled of judgement and she was certain he wore it like aftershave.

'Sit down, Melody.' He swept his arm widely, implying that she had a choice of chairs when the reality was there was just one. 'How are you feeling today?'

Saturated and over people like you dictating how I am, and then there's the toxic medications you tell me to take *for my own benefit*. 'I'm fine, Dr Thomas.'

'Mmmm,' he said, looking over the top of his black rimmed glasses and chewing on the end of a pen. 'You say you are fine but I'm not sensing that you *are* fine. I hear that there was some resistance to taking your medication last night?'

'I keep forgetting that I live my life under a microscope.' Her sarcasm did not go unnoticed, and he scribbled on the page in front of him. Shit, she fell into this trap every week.

'You're feeling challenged.' It was a statement, not a question.

She remained silent. It was like a dance. She would say nothing, he would stare and try to break down her walls, then he would give in and rephrase or ask a different question. Sometimes she gave him what he wanted, other times she couldn't be bothered.

'Are we playing this game again Melody, where you refuse to speak? You do realise that if we can sit here and have a conversation it is so much better for you in the long run.' One unkempt eyebrow raised in anticipation of a reply, and she mentally noted the emotional blackmail.

'Okay, yes, I have been feeling reluctant to take the medication. I feel nauseous and not myself when I'm on it.'

'Who are you without the medication?'

She thought about that and struggled to find words. 'I don't know. What does that even mean?'

'I'll rephrase. Who are you when you take the medication?'

'That's really hard to answer. I just know that who I am when I take it, is not me. It helps with one problem and gives me another.'

'So, what we need to do is find a medication that works for you with minimal side effects. What is the hardest thing about the medication for you? The detachment, nausea?'

'I'm not sure I'll have to think about that.'

'Maybe that is something you can spend some time thinking about over the next week so we can develop a plan. There will be a point when you wean off the medication, I am hopeful of that, but for now our goal is to figure out which medication will work best for you.'

Mel left his office. The reality of the situation was that he held all the power and she always felt like he couldn't get her out of his office quick enough.

We need to see progress before we can consider letting you go home. The words echoed in her head. Home. Where even was home now? The house where her mother would watch her like a hawk and treat her like a fractured child? Her home, full of ghosts, memories, and regret? Or here, this white walled prison that smelled of sickness of the mind.

Mel sat on the floor with the art board balanced on her knee. Apparently, doing art could help release your unconscious memories and aid healing.

Sasha, a twenty-two-year-old wellbeing resident started making strange noises while sat at the table. Mel liked Sasha despite feeling quite intimidated by her when they had first met. Sasha was punky looking with piercings and cropped hair that was shaved at the sides. She wore a lot of black eyeliner, and she was covered in tattoos. When Mel got to know her a little better, she found Sasha to be a shy and self-deprecating woman who had experienced a lot in her life, mostly abuse. Sasha struggled to express herself and would become overwhelmed and flip out. She had been in and out of hospital since she was eighteen and she'd suffered numerous traumas that had started in childhood. Mel had learned during group activities that the brain reached almost ninety percent of its adult size by the age of three and exposure to trauma in childhood could change the way the brain develops. The same could be said of experiencing a trauma in adulthood, but there was less chance of changes being permanant, complex trauma from childhood was harder to overcome though. Mel considered herself lucky compared to some in here and she never thought she'd say that. Mel had a diagnosis of reactive depression and anxiety. Most in the Wellbeing Clinic had personality disorders alongside depression or PTSD.

Mel focused on her painting which wasn't turning into the masterpiece she'd planned. She couldn't paint for shit, but tried, nonetheless. The room they were in was basic with white plastic chairs, easels, and worktops full of every coloured paint you could think of. The walls were painted with the colour *Italian chiffon,* which was supposed to be uplifting and make people happy. To Mel, it just looked yellow.

'I've painted you,' Lee said, causing her to jump.

Lee was in his late twenties and ready to go home this week. He was like a different person now that his freedom awaited him.

'That's nice. I think,' Mel said, feeling a little awkward.

'Do you want to see it?' he asked.

Not really. 'Sure.' She walked towards his easel, uncertain what to expect. Mel looked at the painting, which was extraordinarily good. She was taken back by the reflection of herself. Her blue eyes were the focal point of the portrait, and despite them standing out against her shoulder length dark hair and pale skin, the thing that struck her was the pain that her eyes held. Her cheeks are full and lifted. She was intrigued by the woman in front of her, she looked quite beautiful. Mel felt weird seeing beauty in a picture of herself. She wished the mirror could be as kind.

'Do you like it?' Lee asked.

'I... I love it. I mean, you have an incredible talent. I never knew you could paint like this. In fact, I don't know anyone who can paint like this. I think you've been very kind to me though, I don't look like that in real life.'

'But you do. I've sat opposite you for weeks and I've painted what I see before my own eyes.'

'Can we swap eyes?' she said in a bid to ease her embarrassment.

He blushed. 'It's a gift for you. To say thank you for just accepting me, even when I choose not to engage, and for when I did and overshared.'

'Oversharing is celebrated in here, you did good and you're getting out,' Mel said.

'It will be your turn soon.'

'I hope so. Thank you. The painting—it's very kind of you.' Mel wasn't entirely sure she wanted a picture of herself or a reminder about her time in here, but nor could she reject it.

Mel continued to take the medication but felt as if she was swapping one set of issues for another. Her mind felt like a dandelion on the wind: fractured, separated, all over the fucking place. The thoughts of harming herself and the dark depression faded, but it was like seeing the world through frosted glass; all colour, smell, and light dimmed just enough to feel out of reach. Her movements mimicked a battery-operated toy running out of juice. Slow, stilted, and lazy. Her brain forgot how to function regularly. Her family and the few visitors she allowed would struggle. They asked her things and then assumed she couldn't be bothered to answer them. If only they knew the living hell of being trapped in a mind that had slipped into the murky depths of hibernation.

Every Tuesday, her sister visited in the afternoon. She brought things like ice cream which got labelled with Mel's name and placed in a fridge somewhere out of sight. She had to ask a nurse to get it for her; not demeaning at all, no sir! She also got a heap of magazines that had already been read and lots of chocolate.

'I need some nail clippers, Ari. Can you or Mum bring me some?' Mel asked.

Ari bit her lip nervously. 'We can't babe, we signed the papers to say we wouldn't bring anything in that could cause harm.'

'Wow.'

Ari shifted uncomfortably in her seat. Her chest turned red which meant she was stressed.

'You think I'm going to hold the staff up with a fucking nail clipper? Really, sis?'

'It's not my rule, Mel.' The tension filled the air between them. 'You have to understand how unfair it is to ask me to do this.'

Mel laughed. 'Holy mother of God. It's a nail clipper. That's all I am asking for. Not a gun or a knife: a pair of fucking nail clippers. Nail. Clippers.'

Ari stood, her lips a thin line of disapproval as tears threatened to spill from her eyes. 'I'm going. I don't know how to deal with you when you're like this.'

Mel wished she could feel sorrow, but she was hollow inside. She looked at her sister blankly and turned away, too tired to speak.

❖ ❖ ❖

They sat in a circle, six of them including two facilitators. Grant, who was a new resident to the wellbeing clinic, Mel and Carly who have been here for months, Angie the psychologist, and Maya the psych nurse. Angie and Maya sat with their hands on their laps, smiles painted on their faces like masks.

'Now that we all understand why we are here and the importance of being able to share our stories, who would like to go first?' Angie asked in her voice barely above a whisper.

Silence sat between them all like a chasm. Mel quite liked the silence, but she could sense Carly and Maya didn't. This was Mel's eighth group session and so far, she had not followed the plan, according to Dr Thomas. She wanted out of here and in order to tick the boxes she had to participate in all therapy sessions.

'I'll go,' Mel said, keen to get her story out of the way and *participate.*

'Thank you, Mel. Start whenever you are ready.'

Mel felt ten eyes boring down on her and she looked at the floor. 'It was a warm day, quite hot actually by England's standards. My daughter, who was three, begged me to have a swim in the lake

. I gave in and we ended up swimming for longer than intended and by the time we got out of the water we were both shivering. That night she had a slight fever but nothing to get too concerned about. Kids are always sick at that age, right?'

Mel stopped and tried to breathe away the anxiety growing in her upper body. 'The following day, my daughter really wasn't herself and she lay on the sofa most of the day but by evening she'd picked up a little...'

Mel felt the darkness grabbing at her insides as her heart ricocheted around in her chest. 'I can't.' She pushed her chair back and fled the room.

When she woke, she made her way to the window. The clouds hung heavy in the air, and she wondered how they didn't just fall to the ground in defeat. Lord knew she felt like doing it herself. She took some sleeping meds yesterday after the group event and today her mind was overrun with impermanent thoughts. They were there, then gone as if playing hide and seek. She struggled to make sense of much on days like this and spent most of her time doing crossword puzzles or jigsaws, a non-committal process that allowed time to tick away into another day, when things might feel different.

The door opened after a quick knock, which annoyed her. 'Hi Mel, just wondered if you wanted to come and do some yoga? The instructor is here but no one has turned up.' Jane leant against the door frame waiting on a response. Jane was one of the social workers and she loved groups of any kind.

'I don't think yoga is my thing.' Her voice sounded as hollow as she felt.

'Well why don't you come and try it for fifteen minutes and if you don't like it you can leave?' Jane looked at her nails nonchalantly. 'Dr Thomas would be happy to hear that you attended. I could mention it to him tomorrow.'

Mel couldn't help but smile. 'I'll get changed and be out in a minute.'

The activity room smelled of burnt wood and mandarins. A woman with a vibrant white smile and a kind face greeted her. Her name was Ruby and Mel thought she sparkled like one.

Mel positioned herself on the mat as Ruby talked her through different poses during the class. At the end of the session Mel lay on her back and closed her eyes as instructed while listening to the hypnotic sound of Ruby's voice.

'Did you enjoy your class, Mel?' Ruby asked afterward.

'I did. I think this is the first time I have truly felt relaxed in...' She stopped, aware of when it had all changed. 'In a long time. I will definitely come to your class again. Thank you.'

Mel slept well that night. She still woke up during the night, but there were no horrific nightmares and her mind felt clearer. A tiny glimmer of hope opened within her. Small, but there.

Yoga became Mel's new hobby. When there were no classes to attend, she followed the print outs that Ruby gave her and, in a few weeks, could feel a real difference in her body and mind. She changed her eating and rather than reaching for comfort food she opted for healthier options. All of which was noted in a positive light by the people around her. It felt like a fog lifting ever so slowly. Her mood was brighter, she rose earlier in the morning, and she felt as if she was coming out of the darkness.

On the fourth of December Mel left the Wellbeing Centre. She returned to her mum's house with a renewed sense of hope for the future.

CHAPTER 5

— · —

MEL

It was nine am on Christmas morning when Mel opened her eyes and looked at her watch. She was in no hurry to get downstairs, so she wrapped the quilt tightly around herself and lay on her side. The smell of the turkey cooking curled under her door as if to entice her. It did smell good, and it was making her hungry so she slowly ventured downstairs.

'Merry Christmas,' she said, kissing her mum on the cheek.

'Merry Christmas, darling. I know I've said it a few times but it's lovely to have you home. I did miss you.'

'Just a few?' Mel mused as she curled herself up on the sofa, the soft sound of Johnny Mathis in the background adding to the festive atmosphere.

'Darling, would you like a bacon sandwich and a nice cup of tea?' Grace asked.

'Yes Mum, that would be lovely.' She wrapped her dressing gown tightly around her even though the heating was on. Maybe it stemmed from being in the womb, but Mel found it so soothing to be wrapped up and that was why winter was her favourite month. She flicked through the TV channels and settled on Scrooge, another Christmas Day tradition.

Her mum walked into the lounge and placed her breakfast on the coffee table in front of her.

'Thanks mum, the house smells delicious. I can't wait for lunch.'

A short while later Mel walked into the kitchen. Mel looked at her mum, her face flushed with the chaos of Christmas, and she knew that her mum, Grace, loved this day of multi-tasking. The turkey was cooking while Grace glazed homemade mince pies and then peeled vegetables. Christmas television was on in the background, and it felt festive, despite there being two very important people missing. Ella and her dad.

At twelve o clock on the dot Grace poured herself a sherry and placed some walnuts and hazelnuts in a bowl along with a pair of nut crackers. It was a tradition that her dad had started, and her mum continued to offer them up even though no one ate them. It did seem fitting though, like the star on top of the Christmas tree.

Ari and Jay arrived just after twelve and they exchanged gifts.

'Here you go, Mel.' Ari handed her a gift. Mel looked at the small box wrapped in black and gold paper, tied with ribbon. So much effort and thought had gone into that. She felt bad because her gifts were wrapped without much care and finished off with a stick-on bow. She opened the box and gently unfolded the black tissue. Inside lay a dainty silver anklet with a tiny feather hanging from it.

'Thank you, Ari, it's beautiful.' They shared a hug and then she watched Ari open the gift she had given her.

'Here you go, you two.' Grace handed them each an identical festive bag. They both laughed, remembering their childhood when they would often get the same thing but in different colours. Her mum used to insist it was to avoid arguments, but they had both hated it.

'Okay let's see what we got sis,' Mel said as she pulled out an envelope with money in, some bath bombs, chocolates, a movie gift card, a book, and some new slippers.

Mel and Ari gave Grace her joint gift which was a coffee machine that she had been eyeing up for a while.

'The table looks beautiful, Mum,' Mel said as she eyed the flickering candles, acorns, and baubles that adorned the red table runner that sat in the centre of the table. Each dinner plate sat on a gold placemat with a napkin parcel. On each napkin sat cutlery, and on top of that a sprig of holly and a name tag, tied loosely with a red velvet ribbon. There was a mix of the earthy nutty aroma from the acorns and holly and a hint of cinnamon from the candles. 'It smells like Christmas,' Mel said to herself, and smiled.

They ate a traditional dinner of turkey, roast potato, parsnips, sprouts and carrots with cranberry sauce, before they lazed around watching TV until they had room for dessert.

'Come on then, let's get our coats on and get this over with,' Grace said as she stood up.

'Do we have to mum? It's freezing out there.' Ari screwed her face up in protest.

'It won't take long, come on.'

They walked to the sea front, the wind flicking up spray onto their lips while cutting through their layers of clothing. They were all quiet. Mel knew they were thinking about her dad. She couldn't remember a Christmas day since they had moved when they had not done this walk. Her dad used to say it did them good to get out of the house and have some fresh air, when the reality was it was really an excuse for him to call at the pub on the way home. She smiled at the memories and felt a sense of trepidation at how quickly time passed. This year for the first time they decided against the pub and opted for hot chocolate and their favourite Christmas movie, *The Holiday*, while snuggled up on the sofa, in front of the fire.

Ari and Jay left after the movie, and after eating too much Mel went to bed with her new book. Today had been a good day and she felt grateful to be back home with her family.

It was early February and outside looked like a winter wonderland. Mel traced a picture of a snowman in the condensation that had gathered inside the bedroom window. It took her back to her childhood and images played out of her and Ari laughing as they took clothes out of their dad's wardrobe. Him coming home to find his gloves, hat, and scarf on the snowman they had spent an afternoon building. He'd introduced himself to the snowman calling him sir and had then proceeded to compliment his scarf, commenting how he had one the same. They had been in fits of laughter, fully believing that their father had no idea that they were his items. It felt like seven lifetimes ago that the world had been that innocent.

'Why would you want to go out when it's so cold?' Her mum was wringing her hands together as if Mel had just told her she was about to throw her life savings into a crowd.

'Because I can't stand being cooped up in here, that's why and the fresh air will do me good. And you know when we were kids you used to tell me and Ari to get outside and play in the snow? Why the change now that I'm an adult?'

Her mum's eyes dropped towards the ground and her shoulders sagged in defeat. She'd lost weight and looked so much older. Mel was very aware that she was the cause of that.

'I'll be fine, Mum, really. I'm just going out for some air.' Her voice was softer now, her way of apologising without saying the word sorry.

'Would you like me to come with you?'

'If you don't mind, I would rather go alone.'

Mel stepped out in the white world of sparkles and breathed in the cold air as her eyes adjusted to the brightness. She loved how the air felt so much cleaner after snowfall, as if each falling flake grabbed pollution on the way down, removing toxins from the atmosphere. There was silence all around her. Her boots punctured the soft white powder beneath her, omitting the occasional squeak as the weight of her body compressed the snow. She had been out of the wellness clinic for almost nine weeks, and she treasured the peace and freedom of having no one else around. For the first time in years, she felt grateful to be alive and well.

Later that evening, Mel braced herself realising that there was never going to be a good time to share her news. She was spending the night with her sister and had hoped the wine would make this easier.

'I went back home,' Mel said. 'You know, before I went into the hospital when I first stayed out the night, that's where I was, the house.'

'Home as in the lake house?' Ari asked, eyebrows lifted in surprise.

Mel nodded.

'Wow. How was it? How did you feel being back there?'

'It was suffocating. The air was so thick in the house I struggled to breathe.' Mel sighed. 'Everywhere I looked I saw pictures of my past that were so clear it made me forget, for a few seconds anyway.' Tears ran a familiar race down her cheeks.

'Oh, Mel. It will get better, one day it will. I promise.'

Mel felt the poison climb out of its hiding place and flood into her throat, desperate to pour out in the form of words. She hated when people told her that *it would get better*. 'Will it, Ari? When? I've been waiting for two years for it to get better. It hasn't got better and that is why I am going away.'

'Do you mean you're going back to live at the house?' Ari asked.

'No. I mean I'm going to travel.'

Ari's mouth set in a firm line. 'You're joking? I mean, you must be. You've not long been out of hospital. This will tip Mum over the edge.'

'Don't you see that's exactly why I have to go? My life is not my own. I can't leave the house without texts and phone calls. You, Mum, I know you care and mean well but you smother me with questions day in, day out. Where are you, Mel? How are you, Mel? And the reality is you don't want to hear the truth because it terrifies you and neither of you know what to say. You skirt around the past like you're about to step on a snake. I need some space to breathe, sis.'

Ari opened her mouth as if she was about to object, but she remained silent.

'I don't mean that to sound harsh,' Mel said, 'I know you love me, and I love you both, but I need to get away so that I can heal fully.'

As she lay in bed Mel smiled to herself. She felt such relief, having got that out of the way. Ari would tell her mum and there would be several discussions before she set off on her adventures, of that she was sure, but she would deal with that. She felt like a caged animal about to be released and she could not wait.

CHAPTER 6

—·—

GRACE

Graced eyed her daughter with concern as she walked into the kitchen.

'Ari darling, how are you?' Something was troubling her; a mother knew these things. 'Is it Mel?' She felt her body hold on to her breath longer than it should have and poured a coffee for Ari while mentally preparing herself for bad news. The result of life turning the tables on your family was that you came to expect the worst. Her therapist said it was a defence mechanism to protect herself.

'She told me yesterday that she'd been back to the house,' Ari said.

'Okay.' Grace handed Ari a tea. 'I guess that was going to happen at some point. I don't understand why you are worried though.'

'After we talked, she told me that she's leaving.'

'Leaving?' Grace asked, confused.

'She's going to travel. She said how suffocating we are and how her life is not her own. She got upset, so I didn't ask her any more about it, and now I don't know how to bring it up with her. She still seemed so angry at us.'

'Maybe she was just reacting to having been back in the house. Where would she even go? She's never been past Cumbria, except for her honeymoon. It will all be forgotten about today, I'm sure of it.' Grace said the words with way more conviction than she felt, ignoring the sickness in her stomach.

A car door closed, and Mel walked in looking stronger and more determined than Grace had seen her look for a long time.

Her insides wrapped around themselves.

'Hi,' Mel said as she looked between the two of them. 'Did Ari tell you I'm going travelling?' Her tome was soft but determined.

Grace wanted to shut Mel down and tell her she was talking nonsense, that she wasn't going anywhere. The mother that she had become since Mel was ill, however, was figuring out how to respond without saying the wrong thing.

'You're allowed to speak, Mum. You can ask me things and I won't fall apart.' There was no malice in Mel's voice.

Ari stood up. 'You can't leave the country, Mel. That's the stupidest thing I've heard you say. What if you get sick and no one understands your background?'

Grace cringed, though Ari had made a valid point.

'Do you think the same, Mum?' said Mel.

Grace could hear tension in Mel's voice. 'Let's stop this. Please, I don't want any arguing today.' Grace paused, hoping silence would make it all disappear. 'I'll make us a cup of tea.' She saw Mel's eyes roll as the words left her mouth.

'A goddamn cup of tea is not going to change my life, Mum!'

'Okay. Then tell me what this is all about. Tell me how going to another country will change anything that's happened?'

'I need to leave. I can't stay here anymore. If I stay away from *the house*, I'm running from it, and if I go there, it's too overwhelming. I know it doesn't make sense to either of you, but I really need to do this.'

'Where will you go?' It was the hardest question Grace had ever asked her daughter. She was torn between setting her free and keeping her caged. 'And how often do you plan on staying in touch because it's only natural that we will worry about you?'

'I'm going to travel, for at least a month, maybe longer. My plans are vague at this stage but I'm flying to India, and who knows from there.'

'This is ridiculous! You don't even have a plan!' Ari's said. 'I never had you down as this selfish, Mel. As if Mum and I haven't been through enough worry with you, now season three is about to start up.'

The statement hung in the air between the three of them.

'Have you heard yourself, Ari?' said Mel. 'Do you listen to the words that come out of your mouth? And if you do, what the hell is wrong with you? Do you have any idea how it feels to know I am a burden to you both?'

Ari gawked in disbelief. 'I have never said you were a burden, Mel.'

'The thing is, every time you remind me how worried you are, how worried Mum is, you are telling me exactly that. I know you care but all of this...' Her arms expanded between them. 'It's too much and it's adding to the weight I already carry, hence why I need to escape for a while. I don't expect you to understand because this grief and this journey belongs to me, not you.'

Grace looked at her daughters. She had never seen them so divided. 'That's unfair, Mel.'

'That's what you don't get though, Mum. I want it to be mine. I want to be selfish with this thing I have to carry with me every day. And the reality is, neither of you will ever understand it from my perspective because your story is different to mine.'

Grace had no words. She felt forced to pretend she was supportive of this crazy decision of Mel's to travel to foreign lands. Alone and vulnerable. Mel was an adult and yet Grace felt as if she was dealing with a teenager. The only difference was she could no longer demand that Mel do as she said.

'What will you do there?' Grace asked. 'And before you say anything more about me worrying, it's what mothers do, and I would have been asking you these questions regardless.'

'Sunbathe, swim in the ocean, meet new people. I don't know mum. I guess I want space to breathe and I want to find that adventure for life that I used to have. All I do in between falling apart, is eat, sleep, and work. I want to find myself again. And I can't do it here.'

'Will you tell Carter you are leaving?' Grace immediately realised by the look on Mel's face that she'd stepped on one of those verbal landmines that she was continually trying to dodge.

'Why would I tell him? He's probably on an all-inclusive holiday with the boys.'

Grace felt for Carter. It seemed he could only do wrong. Of course, she couldn't say that to Mel.

'That's fine, Mel, I didn't mean to upset you. Can you at least give us an outline of what your plans are?'

'I'll fly to India, and then maybe Hong Kong. Beyond that is a mystery and that's what's so appealing about it.' Her face was illuminated with excitement and Grace felt such conflicting emotions.

'If it's a break you need, we could go on a holiday,' Ari added, desperation evident in her voice.

'Look, I appreciate your offer sis, really I do, but I really need to go on my own.'

Grace sighed. 'But you've never been out of the country alone, love! You've always left everything up to Carter to arrange.'

'Well, this might be the making of me, who knows. One thing that is guaranteed is that my life cannot possibly be any more of a shitshow than it is right now.' Mel picked her bag up and fished for her keys. 'I'm going to the travel agent. It would be lovely if you could both support my decision, believe it or not, this is not about making either of you worry. And despite what I said, I am grateful for all of your support over the past few years, but something needs to change and only I can make that change.'

Grace and Ari looked at each but remained silent as Mel drove away, aware that neither of them could do a thing to stop her.

CHAPTER 7

— · —

MEL

Mel stepped out of the plane and through the tunnel towards the metal interior of the add on carriage. It looked no different to any other, but the exit into the airport was life changing in so many ways. Mel was in Mumbai on her first ever solo adventure, and it was as equally terrifying as it was exciting.

The airport was eye catching; large white columns fed into vast ceiling panels punctuated with lights. Looking up from the ground up, it was like an enormous white honeycomb sparkling above her. The contrasting brown marble floors and facias gave it a feel of opulence which was not what she'd expected.

Once outside the hot air hit, bringing with it a smell of sunshine, spice, and traffic fumes. After a hair-raising taxi journey from the airport with mopeds, people, and animals walking out into the traffic, Mel breathed a sigh of relief when she arrived at the hotel. Check in was quick and as soon as she dumped her belongings in the room, she messaged her mum and sister to let them know she had arrived safely. The pressure had slightly eased when she told them her friend Jade would be joining her later in the week. Jade was staying for thirteen days so it would be a great way to start her adventure.

She unpacked her suitcase and walked out onto the balcony and her eyes feasted on the sight before her. The Arabian Sea was only a few hundred metres from the hotel, winking at her and summoning her into the azure water. Betel palm trees surrounded the pool and offered shade for the sun loungers scattered in zigzag fashion beneath them. Lush green lawns were being sprinkled with water, while pathways hinted at new adventures beyond the trees to where the eyes could not see. Mel made her way down to the pool, stopping to grab a Long Island iced tea before positioning herself on a lounger, partially in the shade with legs and body out and her face and head under an umbrella.

The sun stroked her skin, and she closed her eyes. *You're in India, Mel. You did it.* She smiled to herself.

'Excuse me, Madam, can I get you anything?' A man asked. He was dressed in brown trousers and a cream short sleeved shirt with the hotel logo sewn on to the breast pocket. He placed her empty glass on the circular tray he was carrying.

'Could you bring me a soda water please?' She quickly scanned the menu. 'Oh, and could I have a vada pav please?' A deep-fried potato patty was not something she would usually eat at home, but it somehow felt exotic to eat one in India, and it did not disappoint when it arrived. Mel spent a few hours relaxing, sipping cocktails and swimming.

After a shower and change of clothes Mel walked into the lounge and ordered herself some food before taking a seat. She sipped her chardonnay and savoured the salted pistachios that had just been placed on the bar. There was a low thrum of chatter coming from the dozen or so people that were in the lounge bar.

Mel turned to her right to the woman who had just ordered wine. She was around five foot eight with a lithe figure, glossy black hair and her beige dress, although simple, just enhanced her overall look. The woman turned and smiled at Mel.

'I'm so sorry,' Mel gushed as she blushed slightly, 'I didn't mean to stare. I was just admiring your hair. And your dress. You look so lovely.'

'Oh, thank you, that's so kind of you. I'm Prisha.' She held out a manicured hand.

Mel discovered that Prisha was an accountant who lived an hour and a half outside of Mumbai in a small village. Once a month she stayed in a hotel in Mumbai because she needed a fix of city life, and it made her feel as if she was on holiday.

'What brings you to India, Mel?' Prisha asked.

'This is the first time I've ever been on holiday alone, but I do have a friend joining me in a few days. Coming to India was a bit of a whim if I'm honest. I'm on a journey, or adventure. Something like that.' Mel waved her hand, trying to come across as someone who did this kind of thing regularly. 'I guess like you, I needed to get away from my hometown.'

'I can relate. I would love to travel to Europe and hope to do so with a husband if I ever find one. So, is coming to India something you have always wanted to do?' Prisha asked.

'My husband and I had always planned to visit India.' Mel swallowed the rest of her wine and Prisha picked the bottle out of the wine cooler and topped up her glass. Time stopped and where words should have flowed easily for Mel, tears took over.

'Oh gosh,' Prisha said, as she looked around helplessly. 'What is it? What did I say? I'm sorry, I didn't mean to upset you. Here, let me get you a tissue.'

Prisha rattled off a conversation with the barman who was looking at Mel with concern, or distain, she couldn't figure it out, but nor could she stop the tears that fell like the first rains of a monsoon. Prisha ushered Mel into a quiet booth away from the bar, and more sobs followed until she felt as if her body were shuddering toward some sort of malfunction. Tissues and drinks were pushed towards her in a clear bid for the episode to subside and after a few gulps of an unknown drink, Mel managed to breathe her way to some form of manageable distress.

'Two years ago, my three-year-old daughter died, and it turned my world upside down, hence why I am here alone and not with my estranged husband. He is actually still my husband believe it or not. We just fell apart and have never discussed making it a permanent thing.' Mel dabbed her eyes with a tissue. 'You're the first person I've told that to aside from a therapist.'

'Oh Mel, I'm not sure what to say.' Prisha shifted in her seat awkwardly but remained attentive.

'Her name was Ella. She was beautiful and so funny, and very smart for her age.' Tears came again in another tidal wave and Prisha was starting to look out of her depth. It seemed the alcohol had unleashed an unstoppable force.

Mel had no idea how long they sat in the lounge but did not resist when Prisha guided her into an elevator and ushered her into her room, where she was helped onto the bed. The curtains were drawn, and blackness filled the room.

Mel woke to darkness, mouth sandpaper dry, head pulsing in pain. She remembered lying by the pool drinking cocktails, and then talking to a Prisha. Flashbacks of Prisha comforting her: cocktails, and tissues, and—how mortifying! She had embarrassed herself immensely on her first day in the country and she had used a total stranger as a grief counsellor. How could she ever go back down there with all those people in the hotel lounge and bar witnessing her meltdown. She lay back down, unable to face neither food nor people and allowed her head to sink back into the pillow.

Sometime later there was a knock at the door. Mel looked through the peephole and Prisha was standing there. Sheepishly, Mel opened the door. Prisha handed her a bottle of water, a warm croissant, and a small box of chocolates.

'I thought you could use these. I hope you don't mind me coming here but I wanted to check that you were okay. I know after I've had a big night, I always worry what others might think of me.'

It was as if she could read her mind. 'I'm so sorry, I'm really embarrassed.' Mel said. 'I don't normally pour my soul out to total strangers. Or break down in a bar full of people.'

'Mel, you have nothing to feel embarrassed about. I feel privileged that you shared your story with me. And don't worry about what other people think, they don't know what you've been through and besides, they were all too interested in themselves to pay you any attention.' Prisha placed her hands together in a loose prayer pose. 'I would love it if you would come to the shops with me in an hour or so, if you feel up to it.'

'Thank you for being so kind to me.' Tears threatened again but Mel managed to stave them off by eating the warm croissant. She had been fortunate to share her story with such a lovely woman. That was the thing with grief that others didn't understand. It was fluid, it didn't show up at set times on demand. It rose out of nowhere like a ferocious beast.

Later that evening Prisha drove them to Juhu, a restaurant overlooking the beach. They bonded and talked as if they had known each other for years while listening to waves crash into the shore.

'Do you mind me asking what happened to your daughter?' Prisha was looking at Mel with large brown eyes, free of judgement.

'Carter and I took Ella into the woods, and she fell and cut herself. The cut wasn't a bad one, but she made a bit of a fuss as kids do. Once we put a band-aid on, though, she was fine. The following day we went swimming in the lake outside our house. That night Ella had a bit of a fever, but I thought it was just a normal child related thing. Kids are always sick at that age, so I gave her Calpol and put her to bed. The next morning, I woke and knew immediately that something was wrong.' Mel stopped as her body remembered the intense feelings of anxiety and terror as a wave of dizziness swept over her.

Prisha bit her lip. 'Sorry, I shouldn't have asked.'

Mel took a deep breath. 'When I woke it was late, the sun was shining brightly in the room, there was no sign of Carter and I looked at my watch. It said exactly three minutes past eight. Carter left for work at six-thirty and Ella had never slept later than six am. I rushed to her room, panic driving me as if I knew what I would find before I arrived. She was curled up, her back towards me and I shouted her name before I got to her. There was no response. I remember a scream leaving my mouth before I'd even touched her. She was a strange colour with bruising on her skin. Ella was rushed to hospital, and they told us that she had sepsis.' Tears rolled off Mel's face and her heart raced but she had managed to say the words without collapsing in a sobbing heap. 'We sat at her bedside for two days and they told us there was nothing they could do.'

Prisha grabbed Mel's hand and squeezed it. She did not try and paper over the grief with platitudes, she simply allowed it to be what it was.

It was the first time Mel had experienced absolute acceptance. She was used to people wanting to make a quick exit, change the subject, or hug her and tell her that *everything would be all right.* 'Thank you, Prisha. Thank you for asking and for allowing me to tell my story without giving me advice or telling me how I should feel.'

'My darling, I would never dream of trying to imagine how you feel. Thank you for being brave enough to share your story with me.'

Mel watched the dragonflies dancing through the air, and she felt a sense of contentment that she had not felt since before Ella died. It felt strange but exciting.

'I know we've only just met Prisha but I feel as if I've known you forever, and given that I've offloaded my life on to you, you probably feel the same.' Mel laughed.

'It's been a blessing and a pleasure and I hope that we can see each other again before you leave the country.'

They walked on to the beach and talked about less intense things as they made their way to the lights of the nearest beach bar, which glistened in the distance. Mel more aware than ever of the sand beneath her bare feet, cool and firm. She had been right to come on a journey, and if today was anything to go by, she was going to have an amazing time.

CHAPTER 8

—·—

MEL

Mel pulled back the curtains and soaked up the view that greeted her. She doubted she would ever get sick of waking up to views of the Arabian Sea and hearing the sound of the birds singing their morning song. Her phone vibrated on the bedside table and she reached for it.

'Yes Mum, I am eating well and no, I've not been sick,' Mel answered her phone, pre-empting her mum's questions.

'Oh, that's a relief, darling. When does Jade arrive?' Grace shouted down the phone as if she was trying to yell to India from Scotland.

'Early hours of tomorrow morning, Mum. I'll message you when she arrives, and when you call me, you really don't need to shout, I can hear you fine.'

Grace shouted her goodbyes to Mel, along with her advice on how to stay safe.

The following morning Mel and Jade left the hotel on the first trip of their holiday together.

'I can't look!' Jade covered her eyes. 'People keep stepping out in front of cars and there's cows walking around everywhere. I thought this was meant to be relaxing.'

'That's what makes it fun.' Mel laughed as she listened to the noise which ricocheted between buildings. There was no escaping it as they travelled by bus with windows open in place of air conditioning.

Jade rolled her eyes and grinned. 'Our idea of fun clearly differs.'

'You just haven't slept enough,' Mel said.

'It was one thirty by the time I checked in and all I wanted to do was knock on your door. I opted to lie in bed and watch the clock tick until three am. I'm too excited to be tired anyway!'

Thirty minutes later, they arrived at the ferry port which was noisy and a little overwhelming. There were carts everywhere the eye could see, selling bangles, food, and ornaments. People were moving around like ants on a mission yelling out instructions to others.

They boarded the ferry to Gharapuri, the village of caves, also known as Elephanta Island, and they sat at the front of the ferry so they could take in the rising sun. The heat was already starting to crank up and Mel was glad that her mum had packed her a battery-operated fan.

'I can't believe we are in India, Mel!' Jade shouted above the noise of the engine.

'It's surreal, isn't it? I feel as if I'm living someone else's life right now. I can't actually believe I made it onto the plane and all the way to India on my own.'

'Me neither, but I'm so glad you did otherwise I wouldn't be here with you right now!'

The sun licked at their skin as they stepped off the ferry and started the walk up the two hundred or so steps. There were more stalls and carts selling ornaments, windchimes, trinkets and souvenirs. Tarp draped above them, forming one large tent to keep the heat of the day from assaulting the visitors. The air held on to the day's warmth that was waiting to be unleashed. Flies were already hovering, waiting to annoy whoever got in their way. Mel locked eyes with a woman who looked to be in her sixties. Her grey hair was plaited and reached her lower back, her eyes sparkled with life and kindness. She exuded beauty.

They reach the top of the steps and stop to catch their breath.

'I'm so unfit,' Jade gasped.

'You're not alone.' Mel looked at the sight before her. 'It was worth it, though. It's hard to believe these carvings have been here since the third century BC. It makes you wonder how they could create something so detailed when the tools would have been so basic. And how did they get up so high? And how amazing that the carvings are still preserved all of these centuries later.'

Jade raised an eyebrow. 'Wow, you're really into this aren't you? Don't get me wrong, it's cool, but I'd much rather be sat by a pool sipping cocktails.'

Mel screwed her face up.

'What's that face for?'

'Oh, I haven't had time to tell you about my cocktail fuelled breakdown when I arrived, have I?' Her cheeks coloured as she thought about it so she changed topic.

'This is a world heritage site and when you are grey and old you will be able to tell your great grandkids about it, so put those cocktails on hold for a few hours and then we will be lounging by the pool. If they serve me that is.'

'Sounds juicy,' Jade said.

'It really wasn't. I want you to meet Prisha though. We're having dinner with her next weekend. You'll love her. She's twenty-four and single. She refused an arranged marriage and her father disowned her, and then he died of a heart attack six months later. We bonded over heartache. She's gorgeous. Five foot eight and a size looks great in everything.'

'Your heartache is a little different to her heartache, babe.'

Mel chose to ignore the comment. 'So, Prisha's mum was beyond devastated after the father died and she told her to forget about the marriage arrangement, she was fearful she'd lose her daughter as well. Prisha works hard and every month she stays in a hotel. I'm excited for you guys to meet; she's making a special trip back and I just know you'll love her.'

'She sounds interesting. And lovely.'

'More interesting than you think. And judging by your face, you're not into these carvings. So, what says we take the ferry back as soon as I've taken some pictures and then we can hire a moped and go see the rice fields? We've still got loads of time and might as well do as much as possible.'

Jade's eyes widened. 'I've never rode a moped before!'

'You can ride a bike, can't you? It's the same thing, relax,' Mel said.

Two hours later, Mel sped off with Jade trailing behind her, hoping the directions she'd been given would get them where she wanted. After riding for an hour or so, Mel stopped at a cluster of houses and pulled off the helmet, her damp hair clinging to it. Dogs lying on the dusty road barked as if competing to see who could go on the longest. It was irritating her and so was the heat. Sweat trickled down her back and her shoulders stung from being exposed to the sun after years of hiding from the Scottish weather.

'We should go back!' Jade shouted above the din of dogs barking.

'I need to find a shop first for water.' The need to drink was so strong that Mel knocked on a random door and waited. She looked at the peeling red paint on the door and wondered if her shoulders would resemble it tomorrow.

A woman with a protruding stomach and long dark hair opened the door. She smiled at Mel and nodded. The whites of her eyes were clear and bright, making her brown eyes stand out. She had a kind face and a permanent smile.

'Excuse me, is there a shop I can buy water?' Mel asked.

The woman tipped her head to the side as if confused and Mel looked inside her house which was nothing more than a square room with everything in one space. One bed was pushed up against the painted concrete wall. Two chairs and a table nestled against the opposite wall, big enough for two dinner plates and not a lot more. There was a basic kitchen that consisted of a stove and four cupboards, a small fridge, and a small bookshelf which was neat and tidy. There was no sign of a toilet and Mel wondered where that might be but thought it best if she didn't know. A brush and mop stood behind the door and although the room was basic, it was very clean.

'Water?' Mel said again tipping an imaginary glass to her mouth. The woman beckoned her to enter her house. Mel turned to Jade, who looked anything but amused.

'What do you think you're doing?' Jade whispered. 'Your mum will string me up if I tell her you're going into strangers' houses, Mel.'

'So don't tell her.' Mel muttered loud enough for Jade to hear.

'Please.' The kind woman pointed to a seat.

Mel sat down awkwardly, unsure what she should do. She watched the woman pull a bowl from a cupboard and then lift a lid off a pan sitting on the stove top. The smell of curry filled the air. The woman placed a bowl of rice and curry sauce in front of Mel and pushed the food towards her.

'Please.' The woman put her hands to her mouth to encourage her to eat. Mel squashed some rice into her fingers because there was no cutlery and ended up with curry halfway up her hand just as Jade took a picture of her. The woman beckoned for Jade to come and join her.

'Please.' She pointed to the free chair opposite Mel and served another bowl of food. She poured them a glass of water from the fridge and placed it next to them. Mel watched the condensation trickle down the glass as she pushed the food into her mouth, surprised at her hunger.

'So, I guess you'll be spending tomorrow on the toilet,' Jade muttered.

Mel was embarrassed as she looked into the kind eyes of the woman who had invited them into her house.

'Do you even know what you are eating?' Jade hissed.

'You're being so rude,' Mel mumbled.

The lovely host walked toward Jade with a bowl and pushed it into her hands, not giving her any option other than to accept it. Jade glared at Mel and started putting food in her mouth as if she was being held at gunpoint. Mel couldn't help but laugh and she took a picture of Jade, capturing the sheer horror of the situation in her expression. When their bowls were empty the woman brought a dish of water for their hands and a rag to dry them on.

'Thank you so much, that was lovely,' Mel said. The woman smiled and nodded even though she'd probably not understood a word. Mel offered the woman some money, but she shook her head. Mel felt shame wash over her when she thought about the opulent hotel she was staying in. Her bathroom was almost bigger than this woman's house.

'More water? Please?' Mel motioned to the woman. She watched her open the fridge and saw it rock from side to side. Rust patches made it look ready for retirement. Nonetheless, she gulped the cool water down, which was bliss after the curry, and she started to wonder if Jade had been right. Maybe she'd been a bit too hasty, but the woman had been so kind, and the food had been so good.

After thanking the woman again, they both jumped back on the bikes and made their way towards the rice field which had stunning views as the sun started to set. They parked their bikes and sat on a patch of grass and a comfortable silence sat between them as they looked out to the sight before their eyes. Layers of rice fields logged with water sat one above the other, like a huge, mirrored staircase that would not have gone amiss in *Jack and The Beanstalk*. Just visible were the people working there, no bigger than dots in the distance. The sun setting on the fields highlighted the reflections of the water and the different shades of green. It was like stepping into a 3D painting and there was no need for words because it was like nothing either of them had seen before.

Mel thought back to the house they'd just had been in. It was so basic, yet incredibly clean. The food was probably the best she'd eaten, and the woman was so ready to give, yet she seemed to have so little compared to most. She thought about her own house that stood empty. A house with too many rooms, plush furniture, and expensive bedding.

'Penny for them.'

The interruption pulled Mel out of the past. 'Oh, you know, just thinking about how little that woman appeared to have so little, yet she was happy to feed two complete strangers without any hesitation. How many people back home would do that?'

'Mmm, yeah. Not many, I guess. People are too scared to speak to strangers now, let alone invite them into their home.'

'It's sad, don't you think? We've lost the ability to stay connected, to belong to something.'

'Well, everyone is too busy working and doing life to be feeding the street. You're right though, there is a disconnect and it is sad.'

'All the more reason to relish in the beauty and hospitality of this country while we are here, then.' Mel took her camera out to capture the beautiful sight before her.

Jade prodded Mel with her spoon before she dived into her dessert. 'So, tell me about the cocktail incident. I've waited all day.'

They'd decided to stop at the hotel for dinner and have an early night because they were both exhausted after a long and very hot day.

Mel looked around her and flushed. Thankfully it was quiet and there was a different barman on duty. 'When I arrived, the first thing I did was go to the pool and drink a cocktail. One became three or four and next thing I'm in the bar chatting to people.'

Jade snorted with laughter. 'Oh my God, that is so you when you've had a drink. You go from anti-social to socialite in three drinks.'

'Yeah well, it went rapidly downhill from there. I started talking to Prisha and drank some more and then I'm bawling my eyes out in front of everyone. I woke the next morning and couldn't even remember getting to bed. Prisha brought me some breakfast and water and she was so kind. I told her all about Ella and once the floodgates opened... Well, you can imagine.'

'Oh babe, it probably did you good to get it out. You never talk about it and maybe talking to a complete stranger was exactly what you needed.'

'Maybe,' Mel said solemnly.

'I'm feeling like yoga on the beach tomorrow morning. Do you want to join me?' Jade asked.

'Why not? Let's do the half day bazaar tour as well, and if I am getting up at an ungodly hour to do yoga

I'm going to bed to get some sleep.' Mel hugged Jade and then made her way to her room. As soon as she'd brushed her teeth she turned the aircon on and lay on the bed welcoming sleep while counting her blessings to be sharing such a magical experience with her friend.

CHAPTER 9

MEL

The alarm went off at three fifteen am. Mel rolled over and groaned. She phoned Jade as agreed.

'I'm up, I hate you, and I'll see you in thirty minutes downstairs,' Jade croaked before ending the call. Mel laughed.

They boarded the bus and Mel rested her head against the window as they made their way to Mumbai airport for a short flight to New Delhi. It was already thirty degrees and Mel was beginning to regret her decision.

'Do people not wear deodorant in this country?' Jade wrinkled her nose. 'And I can't believe that we are travelling this early in the morning.'

'You can't come to India and not see the Taj!' Mel replied. 'Stop complaining.'

'I'm sure I'll be grateful once we arrive. Sorry for being a grumpy bitch. You know me and mornings.'

'It's fine. It is very hot, so we'll try and keep in the shade and drink plenty of water,' Mel said as she looked out of the window at the chaos outside.

After a short flight they arrived in Agra, New Delhi, and once through the security checkpoint they entered the grounds through the Eastern gate and walked through the gardens which were lined with neat hedges and well-manicured lawns.

The guide bellowed: 'You will soon be coming to the Great Gate, also known as Darwaza-I Rauza and this will allow you the first glimpses of the Taj Mahal.'

The Islamic architecture of the Great Gateway was like nothing Mel had seen before. Terracotta in colour, it stood regally, demanding attention, and whispering secrets beyond its expanse. The domes carved out of the gateway were adorned with tiles and intricate artwork. It was stunning. In the background there was the sound of car horns and the whisper of conversations carried away in the breeze.

'Wow!' Jade said, eyes wide with surprise.

'I know, right?' Mel reached for her camera to capture the beauty, but the pictures did not do it justice.

They entered a shaped archway through the Great Gate. It was dark inside and it was obvious why they had opted to keep it that way, because once you stepped out of it you were in front of the blinding white Taj Mahal. It was so majestic, both Mel and Jade stood silently in awe.

'The Taj Mahal is one of the Seven Wonders of the World,' said the guide, 'and was designated as a UNESCO World Heritage Site in 1983. The white marble mausoleum was built in 1648 by the Mughal emperor Shah Jehan as a memorial to his wife, Mumtaz Mahal.'

'Imagine someone loving you that much that they would build you something as magnificent as this,' Jade said.

Mel nodded silently as she soaked up the view in front of her.

'Taj Mahal houses the tombs of Shah and Mumtaz Mahal.' The guide bellowed.

'I know this guide is giving us useful information, but I really wish he'd shut up and just let us explore on our own. I just find myself in a moment of beauty and then he starts up again,' Jade said.

'Agreed.' Mel said as she looked through the lens at the sight before her.

On either side of each arch there were two upper and two lower dome shaped arches that had been carved into the marble. And each one had square cut-outs with designs etched into them, giving the effect of panelling. The intricate lattice work was beautiful, and it made Mel feel emotional to think of the love this couple must have shared. Memories attempted to push through her mind, lingering like a reflection in a window.

'Hey, are you okay?' Jade snapped her fingers. 'You're miles away.'

'Old ghosts,' Mel said, quietly before walking off to take more pictures.

Their next stop was Agra Fort, a red sandstone fort which took more than eight years to build. It was magnificent and overwhelming in size with a maze of courtyards, chambers, and mosques, but to Mel it was nowhere near as spellbinding as the Taj Mahal. After an hour of walking, they boarded the bus for the last stop today before their flight back to Mumbai.

Sanskrit Gems Market was a shopping heaven, no matter what age. Handicrafts made of marble and sandstone, Persian carpets, brassware, jewellery, artwork, embroidered tablecloths and so much more.

'We could buy some leather slippers as a reminder,' Jade suggested as she entered a shop. Mel hovered outside but the giggling coming from Jade intrigued her enough to go inside and see what was amusing her. Mel watched Jade blushing and twirling her hair as an attractive man tried to sell her jewellery.

'My wares are beautiful,' he said, 'but not quite as beautiful as you.'

Mel took out her camera. It was payback time. 'Sorry to interrupt,' she said with a smirk.

'Mel, come buy something!' Jade gushed, a little too eagerly.

'Can't think why you would need more jewellery.'

'Ssh, don't embarrass me. This is Ishir. Ishir, this is Melody.'

Mel felt herself go red. 'Hi,' she said. 'It's Mel, as she well knows.' Mel's eyes darted to the left towards Jade.

'Another pretty lady, but this one already stole my heart, sorry.' He broke into a big smile and clasped his chest before winking at Jade. 'Ishir means strong and powerful.' He flexed his arms and puffed his chest out.

'I'm not sure I can take much more of this, said Mel. 'I feel like the third wheel here. Can you just buy your necklace and then tear yourself away from the powerful one please?'

Jade scowled at her and waved her hand as if to usher her out of the shop. Mel stood outside and looked around. There were cars and motorbikes parked up on the road opposite in a style that could only be described as haphazard. There were tuk tuks zooming back and forth and a donkey braying as it pulled a cart behind it laden with bags of fruit and vegetables. The road was dusty and the air was dry. She walked over to a cart that had a mixture of water, soda, and canned beer packed into buckets of ice and water. She bought two beers and walked back into the shop.

'Here you go.' She handed Jade a beer. 'As much as I'd love to stand outside melting and sweating, I'd really like to get back on the bus so we can fly back to the hotel which has aircon and a pool.'

'Sorry,' Jade cooed, after she reluctantly said good-bye to her new admirer. 'He's just so gorgeous.'

'You know he just wants a visa, right?'

'Oh my God, you sound like my mum,' Jade sniped. 'You can't deny that he's very good looking.'

'He is, Jade, but how many women do you think he uses those chat up lines on each day?'

'You're too sceptical, that's your trouble,' Jade replied.

Rain hit out of nowhere and everyone scattered to shelter in shop doorways and under canopies.

'It was sunshine ten seconds ago. Where did that come from?'

'Don't worry, it will soon pass. It rains most afternoons, but never for long.' A female voice said from behind them. Mel turned and smiled at a woman who was dressed in a pink sari edged with gold. She had a gold nose ring and a red jewelled Bindi on her forehead. Her long hair was just visible underneath her headscarf, and she smelled of sandalwood. Mel loved how Indian women always looked dressed for special occasions in their saris. As opposed to her own wardrobe, which ranged from old tracky bottoms and worn jeans to 'special occasion' dresses that rarely saw the light of day.

Mel watched the water droplets hit the heat of the road, turning the ground into a giant air purifier as steam rose. The sun came back out, the rain soon a distant memory as humidity turned the air heavy.

The airport was loud and packed full of people jostling for a seat. Some lay on the floor resting and others slept soundly, although Mel had no idea how with a tannoy blaring out information every few minutes. Onboard the plane, she looked out of the window at the city lights below that twinkled like stars in an upside-down world. It was a short flight but being dark the lights were dimmed. Cabin crew walked silently up and down carrying trays with a choice of snacks. She picked a small packet of pretzels and popped the savoury bite into her mouth relishing the taste and hoping the salt would replace some of the sweat she had lost while trekking around.

Her phone pinged and her world stopped momentarily when she looked at the screen.

Hi Mel. I bumped into your mum, and she told me that you're in India. I can't stop thinking about it.

About us. It's just we always planned to go there together, and it feels wrong you being there, me being here. Sorry. Anyway, I hope it's all you dreamed it would be. Take care. Carter. x

Her heart danced a new beat unexpectedly, causing her to squirm in her seat.

'You okay?' Jade asked sleepily.

'I'm fine.' Mel, confused at the initial reaction to the message, closed her eyes in a bid to block out her past.

She woke to a feeling of heaviness, as if something was not quite right. After breakfast she walked from her room to the pool area, her mood stalking alongside her like a shadow.

'Got you a mocktail,' Jade said as she rubbed sun cream into her tanned skin, designer shades perched on top of her head as she lathered her face. 'No premi wrinkles are allowed on this face.' She laughed, but Mel knew she meant it.

Mel looked at the loungers spaced out around the glittering azure pool. Parasols stood to attention between the luxurious beds under the shade of the betel trees. A woman who looked like she'd fallen off the front cover of a magazine sat on the side of the pool, dark hair glossed back into a neat bun. A gold chain hung from her black bikini top and sloped comfortably around her tiny waist. The water rippled like silk as she slid into it. To her left an ibis walked between loungers pecking at the floor, trying to beat the staff who walked the grounds sweeping up. She could hear the rev of boat engines in the background and despite her beautiful location she couldn't help but think of home.

'What's up with you? Holiday blues because I'm leaving tomorrow?'

'Something like that.'

Jade sat up. 'What is it? Tell me, Mel.'

She hesitated, wondering if she should keep it to herself, but memories of the Wellbeing Centre made her think otherwise. 'I'm just trying to decide where to go to next. I'm tempted to go home but the thought of being smothered by my family does not appeal.'

Jade nodded silently.

'I got a text from Carter yesterday, and it's really thrown me.' Mel handed her phone to Jade.

'I knew there was something else bothering you. And it's pretty obvious he still loves you.'

'It's not as simple as that.' Internally she asked herself how he could still love her after the way she had shut him out.

'Why, Mel?'

'What do you mean, why?'

'Well why is it not simple?' Jade asked. 'Why does it have to be complicated? What happened to you guys was devastating, but life goes on.'

Mel felt herself tense. 'Yeah, well, I'd rather not talk about it, thanks all the same.'

'Sorry if I overstepped the mark. I didn't mean to. It's hard to say the right thing sometimes.'

Mel nodded as she watched parakeets fly between the trees. She felt heavy at the idea of returning home but scared at the thought of continuing her travel alone. The bravery seemed to have deserted her. There was also work. She really had no desire to return to her boring job, but she had no idea what else she could do.

'If you could rewind your life back to when you were fifteen years old, what would you do for a living?' Mel asked Jade.

'Okay, that's deep and unexpected. Erm. Gosh, I'm not sure I've even thought about it, to be honest.'

'That's okay, I'm asking you to think now though. If you could relive your life, what career path would you have chosen?'

'Well, I wouldn't have ended up being an estate agent, that's for sure. Career-wise it's as stable as a pair of scales.'

'So, what would you do differently?'

Jade laughed. 'Jesus! It's like being interviewed for a job. I don't know what I'd do. Maybe become a beautician or something like that.'

Mel thought for a moment. 'Actually, I could see you doing that. Why don't you?'

'What? Why don't I go back to school again? Are you crazy?'

'So, in ten years' time you want to be in the same field of work?'

'Well, no, but by then I'll hopefully be married to someone who earns enough and then I can be a stay-at-home mother.'

'Or you could win the lottery. Or you could change your career while you're young enough to do it and have no commitments.' Mel sipped her lemonade while looking at Jade expectantly.

'Anyway, what's with this whole conversation about going back to school and careers?'

'I guess being here has made me think about things I've not thought about before.' Mel mused. You know how you get trapped in that life of *well this is what I do,* and then it feels too hard or too late to change it. Being here, it's made me realise I don't want to go home to the same.'

'So back at ya—if you could rewind the hands of time, what would you be doing workwise?'

'I'd be a teacher.'

'Wow, no hesitation whatsoever,' Jade said. 'So, are you going to do anything about it?'

'Actually, I think I am,' she said, surprising herself.

'Really?' Jade let out a little squeal of excitement and clapped her hands.

'I can't go back to living the same way. I think seeing people here so happy and often they have so little, it's made me feel that life is just passing me by, and I really need to be doing things that I will get some fulfillment from, not just go to work to earn money. Plus, there's the bonus of school holidays still allowing me time to travel if I want to.'

'Well, it seems like you've got it all figured out. So how about we go to the day spa and treat ourselves to a massage and pedicure. And then we can celebrate your new life awaiting you after we say goodbye to your friend Prisha.'

'It will have to be a small celebration, you're up at five for your flight home, remember.'

'Meh, that's why most people sleep on planes, it's because they're hungover.' Jade declared.

Mel laughed and felt a glimmer of excitement at what the future might hold in store for her.

'I should buy Prisha a small gift. Just to say thank you. I know she has promised to come and visit England, but just in case our paths don't cross again I want her to remember how kind she was. Do you want to come to the shops with me?'

Jade placed her hands on her hips while raising her eyebrows. 'As if you need to ask me to go shopping.'

The two of them linked arms as they made their way out of the hotel towards the bustle of the shopping precinct.

CHAPTER 10

— · —

MEL

After hugging Prisha goodbye both Mel and Jade reflected on their time in India as they scrolled through pictures on their phone while eating roti and a selection of curried dishes, both in denial that their joint holiday was almost at an end.

The following morning as the sun was rising, Mel pulled apart from Jade and willed herself not to get emotional. 'Safe trip home, my friend. This has been the best holiday, thank you so much for joining me.'

'Are you sure you don't want to come with me?' Jade asked. 'I know it would make your mum happy.' Jade held her hands together as if in prayer.

'Part of me would love to say yes, but I'm not giving in just yet. I need a little more time to find myself.'

'Where will you go?' Jade asked.

'Sri Lanka or Goa I think,' Mel said.

'How long for?'

'A week, no more than two. If I want to enrol in uni, I will have to enrol and there's a lot to sort so I won't be that far behind you.'

'Okay, babe. Stay safe on your travels and thanks for the best time. See you when you get home.' Jade kissed her goodbye and got into the taxi. She waved until Mel could no longer see her.

Mel's flight the following morning from Mumbai to Kandy in Sri Lanka was two hours and twenty minutes. It was a quiet flight, and as soon as she was through customs, she jumped in the mini bus for her trip to the hotel. She felt a mixture of excitement and nerves at the thought of being on her own, but she had played it safe and booked group trips, much to her mum's relief.

Her room was small but immaculate, the bathroom unlike any other she'd been in. The spa bath sat adjacent to an outward curved window which gave elevated views of the Kandy Forest and made you feel as if you were suspended in mid-air. Mel sat in the bath until the last light of the day fell from the sky and she felt proud of herself for pushing through her fears and adding to her adventures.

The following morning, she took a swim in the infinity pool which overlooked the hills of Kandy and she tried to pinpoint the aromas that surrounded her. There was a definite hint of coconut and mango, and also the sweet smell of tea from the surrounding Ceylon tea fields.

The heat of the day was already causing her clothes to stick like a second skin as she boarded the bus to the elephant sanctuary, and the refreshing morning swim felt like distant memory. The bus was small and full, and she ended up next to a man in his fifties. His wife had died the year before and they had planned to come to Sri Lanka for their thirtieth wedding anniversary.

'It's a bittersweet trip, this one, love,' he said in his brummy accent. 'And what's an attractive lass like you doing here alone? Oh, that sounded bad, didn't it? I'm not chatting you up, love, you can relax. I'll stop talking now. Jean always said I talked to much and never failed to say the wrong thing.'

Mel laughed. 'You're funny. But I'm sorry to hear about your wife. I lost my daughter two years ago. It's been a long journey coming to terms with it. Hence why I'm here. I left India a couple of days ago and this is my stop off before going home.'

'Oh, love I'm awfully sorry. I feel terrible going on about my wife.'

'All grief is valid and just as painful as the next persons.'

'Oh, I don't know about that,' he said.

They sat in a comfortable silence until the bus arrived at the orphanage and the first stop was the fruit feeding area. The air was pungent with the smell of over-ripe fruit and elephant piss. It was like someone turning on a fire engine water hose. The elephants were roaming along the fences being fed by tourists and there were numerous sheds where they wandered in and out to get fed. A man was running back and forward bringing hay and feed, and no sooner did he put it down when elephants descended and off he went again to bring more supplies. His wide bright smile told Mel he loved what he did and it reinforced her excitement about changing her career path.

Mel followed the group to Kallugala Park which was a walking trail in the centre of the sanctuary.

'Isn't it marvellous!' an elderly woman said, as they watched a herd of twenty elephants walk along the pathway towards the river for a bath.

'It really is marvellous, and I feel incredibly lucky to be here,' Mel said with tears of emotion in her eyes. It felt surreal to see the elephants so close, and although they were contained within the sanctuary, there was a real sense of freedom. Mel watched traffic stop to allow the herd to cross the road as they made their way to the river, and she watched the elephants enter the water one by one. A member of staff directed a huge water jet over the top of them as they waded in the water with their trunks and tails swinging happily. It was an amazing afternoon out and Mel wished that she could have shared this time with someone.

They group boarded the bus, and everyone sat in the same seats. Mel found it intriguing how easily people slipped into routines and how conditioned everyone was not to deviate from what is expected; herself included.

She opened her eyes to find her head resting on the man next to her. She sat up, embarrassed. 'I'm so sorry. I've never fallen asleep on someone like that before. It must be the heat and all of that walking.' Her cheeks burned.

He laughed. 'You're fine, love. It was a tiring day, but a great one. Jean my wife, would have loved it there. She was a real animal lover.'

Mel nodded silently unsure what to say to him. She thought about Ella and how fascinated she would have been with the elephants. She also thought about Carter and for a second, she wished it was him next to her on the bus. It felt a little lonely now that she was here by herself, and she was glad she was returning home in a few days. She'd not replied to Carter's text message but now that she was on her own, she was tempted.

That evening, Mel sat in the restaurant and looked at the steaming plate of kukulmas in front of her, a traditional Sri Lankan chicken curry. The smell was divine, and she closed her eyes savouring the moment as she popped the roti bread and curry sauce into her mouth, tasting fennel, cardamon, lemongrass, and the nip of chillies. She swallowed a mouthful of white wine to cool the fire and reached for her phone. Shocked at how natural it felt to text Carter. Surprised when she felt a smile form on her lips.

Hi. Thanks for the text. India was as amazing as I (we) always envisaged. Currently in Sri Lanka before returning home. Mel.

The following morning, the first thing Mel did was check her phone and read the message waiting for her. Her stomach squirmed like a bag of snakes as she read it.

Wow, Sri Lanka and India! I'm sorry I wasn't there with you to see how amazing it was. Send some pics if you get time. Stay safe. Carter x

She wondered whether to keep this thread going or end it now. She thought back to the question Jade had asked about why it needed to be complicated. He loved her, she still loved him.

She still loved him. It hit her like a freight train. She had been drowning in grief to the point that she'd not allowed anyone close to her. She'd been angry at the world, when really, she'd been angry with herself. So angry that she had locked her heart away to avoid ever feeling pain like that again.

CHAPTER 11

— . —

MEL

Two days later, Mel stepped out of the airport and into the embrace of cold Scottish air. It was almost nine pm and her mum was waiting for her.

'Jesus, I forgot how cold it gets here,' she said, shivering in the cardigan that she'd been certain would keep her warm.' Her mum hugged her tightly. For once Mel didn't hurry the occasion along but enjoyed the warm embrace and smell of her mum's perfume. It occurred to her that people could also smell like home.

Mel looked at the fretwork of frost that covered the cars in the carpark and she longed for the sun on her back.

'It already feels like a lifetime since I was lying by the pool. It's hard to believe it was only yesterday, Mum!'

Her teeth chattered as she pushed the words out of her mouth.

'Well, I for one am very happy to have you home in one piece, Mel. I'll run you a hot bath when you get in and you can imagine that you're in Sri Lanka in that fancy spa bath.'

Mel leaned over and hugged her mum and inhaled her perfume. She'd worn the same one for decades and Mel thought the perfume should be renamed *Grace.*

'It's good to be home, Mum.' Mel's breath almost formed the words in the air, it was that cold. The roads were quiet as they drove out of Edinburgh towards Dunbar for the thirty-mile journey and Mel nodded off as soon as they pulled away from the airport, exhausted by the lack of sleep and travel.

She woke the following morning to the sound of her mum clanking around in the kitchen. It was ten o'clock, but she'd still been awake at two am and even when she had slept, it had been restless with thoughts of Carter going through her head. As soon as she stepped on the bedroom floor, her mum was shouting up the stairs that she was waiting to hear all about her holiday. She inhaled the aroma of coffee and toast as she made her way downstairs.

'Morning. I've missed this smell.' She reached for a slice of toast and layered butter on, watching it pool as it melted.

'Don't they have toast for breakfast in India or Sri Lanka?'

'Not that I'm aware of. They seem to eat rice cakes and roti in India and in Sri Lanka they like curry for breakfast.' Mel laughed as her mum pulled a vomit face.

'My goodness, I could think of nothing worse. I like a nice curry, but I could never imagine eating it for breakfast.'

'There's plenty of fresh fruit around too, Mum, so you would be fine.'

Grace gave a look that implied otherwise. 'So, how was it? I'm dying to hear all about your adventures. And I know I said it last night, but I am so glad you are home. I had visions of you being in hospital with terrible diarrhea.'

Mel spat her coffee out. 'Gross. I'm eating breakfast here.' She started laughing and her mum joined in.

'It was fantastic Mum. There's so much colour everywhere in India, from the saris the women wear to the markets that are full of baskets of different coloured chillies, spices, fruits. And the smells—you just want to eat all the time because wherever you go there is food. Carts are lined up on the side of the road and there's even people selling fruit from long boats on the beach.'

'I hope you didn't eat from a cart! You do look well though, darling. Sunkissed skin suits you, and you look as if you've put a little weight on.'

'That would also be the cocktails me and Jade devoured on top of the food.'

'I'm so pleased you had a nice time. Your sister missed you.'

'I can't wait to tell her all about it.'

'When do you go back to work darling?' Grace asked.

'Urgh, do you have to ruin the mood?' Mel put her head on the cold marble work surface in a bid to deny reality. 'I go back on Monday.' She lifted her head and looked around at the immaculate kitchen, everything in its place, neat as a pin and it reminded her of the routine of work, home, sleep and the reason she had wanted to escape. 'Did I tell you about the day Jade and I hired mopeds?' she asked, trying to avoid a conversation about work.

'No, you did not. I asked you not to do that. I watched a tv show once and the amount of people that were stranded in hospitals overseas due to moped accidents was horrific.'

Mel rolled her eyes. 'Anyway, we hoped on our bikes and after we'd been riding for what felt like hours in the blazing heat, I knocked on a door to ask where I could buy some water because it was so hot. I met the kindest women ever, Mum. Her house was about the size of this room. She had so little and yet she gave what she had willingly, without any hesitation. We ate the best curry and Jade took a few pictures. I'll show you later.'

"Mel! You went into a stranger's house and ate their food! You could have ended up in hospital.'

'Don't be so dramatic, Mum. You're missing the point. Her kindness and the open invitation into her home without hesitation was so natural to her.'

'Stupid if you ask me, there's no way I would ever allow a stranger in here, let alone feed them. Imagine! I'd have a line up at the door every day.'

'Well, that's where we are different because if I had my own house I would, and maybe I will when I move out.'

'Thank goodness that's not on the cards then, or you'll need an extra job for your food bill.'

'Actually...' Mel tapped her fingers on the worktop, equally excited and nervous to break the news. 'I've asked Jade to find me somewhere. It's time I moved on with my life again. You've been great mum, you and Ari, and I can't thank you both enough, but I have to step back out into the world of the living. I'm just renting though, and I won't be far, so you'll still get sick of seeing me.'

Her mum smiled. 'Wow, the holiday has made an impression on you.'

'There's more.' Mel clapped her hands like an excited child. 'I'm going to retrain as a teacher.'

'Wow!' her mum said. 'I think that's a fantastic idea, but how will you afford to live if you're studying?'

'I have savings and I'm going to ask Carter to sell the house.' There was a pause in conversation and silence sat between them for a moment.

'If you feel ready for that, then you have to do what's right for you, sweetheart.'

'I'll be around for a few weeks yet but thanks for understanding.'

Mel's thoughts drifted to the conversation she was yet to have with Carter and her stomach tensed in anticipation. She poured herself another coffee and switched on her computer and typed in the University course she wanted to enrol on. 'Here's to new beginnings.' she whispered to herself.

CHAPTER 12

—·—

MEL

Although time had passed, in some respects it was still frozen. Mel parked her car and looked at the metal railings and large ornate gates, open wide as if to welcome people in. Trees lined the railings to hide the sadness behind the grand entrance.

It had been raining and Mel wondered whether the clouds were programmed to dampen the area several times a day, because it always seemed to be wet here. She walked along the path, the moss slippery beneath her feet and the smell of earth strong in the air. She focused on a few daisies that were pushing through the grass. Anything but look up and take in the enormity of the cemetery.

She only came here twice a year. Some people would never understand that, but she got no comfort at all from sitting at a graveside. In fact, it depressed her and made her incredibly anxious. Instead of thinking of happy memories of Ella, she would think about her lying in the ground alone and it was just too much for her.

A dragonfly darted above her like a firework, its colourful wings disappearing out of sight before catching her eye again. For a moment, it took her mind off the sadness of the day, but the closer she got to the grave the slower her legs worked, making her feel as if the path was growing in length before her.

She stood in front of the gravestone and read her daughter's name, written in gold. She placed her hand on the cold marble to steady herself and slipped a small gold bear beneath the gravel, a gift from mother to daughter that only they would know about. Tightness crushed her chest as the swell of emotion pushed to break free. At first, she tried to fight it, but the pain, guilt, and sadness erupted.

A hand touched her shoulder. Her heart galloped as her feet slipped from under her in fright.

'Sorry. I'm sorry I didn't mean to scare you. I just couldn't watch you and do nothing.' A familiar voice said.

Mel turned to see Carter, teddy bear in one hand, pain etched on his face, tears in his eyes. He held out a hand and pulled her up. Her eyes scanned his face, noting the slight growth of stubble. He hadn't shaved, yet she could smell his aftershave and instinctively she felt pulled toward him, but she stood rooted to the spot. He looked as handsome as ever and he'd lost a little weight because the jeans he wore were the ones she'd bought him, and they hung a little looser than they used to.

'Can you believe she would be five today?' he whispered, as if they were sharing a secret.

He remembered.

'How long have you been here?' She wiped her eyes and looked at him and felt shame wash over her. Of course he would remember today. Why wouldn't he? Ella had been his daughter too and yet she stood here protective, angry at him for intruding, and she wondered at what point she had honoured herself with the title *Chief of Grieving*.

'Long enough,' Carter said. He reached out to her, his hand hovering as if she might vanish. Tears spilled as they gravitated towards each other, his embrace a safe space.

She had no idea how long they stood there frozen in time, bonding over their shared pain. 'I have to go.' Mel pulled away from him, embarrassed and comforted all at once. Carter grabbed her hand as she turned to walk away, causing goosebumps on her skin.

'Let's have dinner. Or a walk. Something, Mel. Please. I don't want to be on my own today.'

'I'll message you soon.' She felt terrible, he looked so deflated. 'I will message you. I promise.'

Mel sat in her car, contemplating. Part of her wanted to go back to him to share memories of Ella and cling to the past together. The other part of her wanted to keep a wall up. As her car pulled out of the cemetery and onto the road, she looked at the rain-slicked road in her mirror, and she told herself Carter needed time alone to grieve.

CHAPTER 13

— · —

CARTER

Carter smiled to himself as he read the text from Mel, while at the same time his stomach knotted together like a frown.

Can we meet?

Nerves. He was nervous at the thought of meeting his own wife, even though they'd been separated for years. Wait, what if she no longer wanted to be his wife? Fuck! He breathed in for a count of four and out for a count of six, just like the psychologist had taught him. This was big. It was the first time Mel was willing to talk to him since she left after Ella died.

He picked up the photograph on his desk. They'd been on holiday in Malta. Mel hadn't wanted to go, she said it was all rocks and not much else and not the kind of place you take children, but he'd convinced her by offering to book everything. All she had to do was pack a case.

They'd stayed in Golden Bay, Mellieha, surrounded by bays and islands, making each day a new adventure. The photograph on his desk was of the three of them on the beach, sun setting in the background. He could almost smell the rotisserie chicken stuffed with herbs wafting from the hotel kitchen. He had Ella in his arms and Mel had one arm around him and they all looked so happy and healthy. It had been one of the best holidays they had ever had.

For the millionth time, he wondered how their life could have changed so drastically. He replayed the morning over in his mind. The one time he needed to leave early and didn't bother to wake Ella. She was always up early, bright eyed and full of questions. He'd loved this time of day with her, she was so inquisitive and easy to please. As long as you were talking to her, she was happy. That morning, he quickly checked through his paperwork, grabbed his briefcase after sinking a cup of coffee, and he left. The number of times he'd berated himself, wondering if the outcome would have been different if he'd gone in to say good morning. He would have seen that she was unwell and that extra two hours could have been the difference.

His heart sat like a rock in his chest, solid and broken. His psychologist told him it did no good to ruminate about what could have been. How the fuck did you stop doing that when you felt you were to blame? He was the one who had insisted on the forest walk and that was where Ella had fallen and cut herself.

Carter was wearing Mel's favorite aftershave and he'd changed his outfit twice. She used to tell him that she loved him in a suit, but that would be too formal and pretty obvious he was trying too hard to impress her, so he'd changed into jeans and a jumper. He sat on the picnic bench with his back to the car park, waiting. He watched a squirrel run along a branch before jumping out of sight. His thoughts automatically slipped into thinking how Ella would have loved to see that. The sky was gloomy and overcast, threatening rain, possibly sleet. He was thankful he had put a thick jacket on.

The crunch of feet on gravel behind him sent his insides into a dance, and the smell of her perfume arrived ahead of her.

'Hi,' Mel said, her voice wavering as she fidgeted with her hands.

'Hi. I didn't think you would get in touch. I'm glad you did though,' he added a little too quickly.

'I thought we should talk properly.'

He swallowed down his fear. 'Before we talk, can I say something?'

Mel nodded; eyes fixed on him.

'I want to say sorry,' Carter said, his voice croaky with emotion.

'For what?'

He looked at the ground and closed his eyes, the weight of his words rendering him silent for a minute. 'I'm sorry for suggesting we go on that forest walk. You said it wasn't a good idea after the rain and I should have listened.'

'Carter...' Mel reached for his hand, and a pulse of electricity travelled up his arm as they touched. 'I could say the same for the lake and it's more likely she got the bacteria from the water.'

'But...'

'No, Carter. You have to stop punishing yourself. It's taken me so long to stop blaming the both of us. My therapist said that if we tell ourselves stories often enough, we start believing them to be true, and neither of our stories are true. It was unfair, devastating, a one in a million, but it wasn't either of our faults.'

Hearing those words and forgiveness crumbled his resolve. He felt her arms fold around him and they cried together. It wasn't the scenario he'd planned when thinking about their meet up. They now sat side by side with the silence drawing the air tighter around them, pulling them towards each other like magnets. He turned to look at her and examined her face. Her blue eyes stood out against her dark, wet lashes. She was still as beautiful as the day he'd met her and the thought of not having her in his life terrified him.

'I want us to try again. I still love you, Mel.'

Mel's eyes brimmed with tears, and she brushed them away. 'Carter, I don't know that I can step back in time.'

'Then we'll step forward.'

'Things are different now. We're different. Wouldn't it be going backwards?'

'We don't have to rewind, Mel. You talk about the stories we tell ourselves, well who's to say we can't rewrite ours?'

A large dalmatian ran past them, followed by a couple dressed in matching wax jackets and wellies. 'Morning!' they waved, before calling after the dog that was nowhere to be seen.

'Don't you want that?' Carter asked her.

'What, matching jackets and boots?' Mel smiled, and they looked at each other. His head was fit to burst with a mixture of memories and things he wanted to say, but he was afraid of saying much more in case he frightened her off.

'Tell me everything. I want to understand what you've been through, even if it's not what I want to hear. Please, Mel.'

'Okay. But not here, it's too cold. Let's go somewhere else,' Mel said.

'Where would you like to go?' Carter asked.

'Do you have the keys to the house?'

He stalled, unsure if going back there was a good idea. 'Erm, I do. Are you sure you want to? I mean I've been staying there on a weekend—the therapist suggested it might help me face things, but it's not what I'd call ready for visitors and it's a long drive.'

'It will be fine. I'll stop somewhere and get some food. You drive straight to the house.' He didn't hesitate just in case she changed her mind, but a part of him wondered if this was Mel's way of ducking out. Would she even turn up? It was a long drive. He had little option but to trust her, so he drove towards their past, hoping that it might just lead them into the future.

As he pulled into the driveway, nostalgia hit him. Five years ago, they had both stood on this spot to stare at the shell of their house that was under construction. They'd not long been married, and they'd spent hour upon hour choosing the kitchen, bathrooms, and flooring. At the time it has been their forever home, so they had made sure the configuration would also work when they had children. The plan had been to wait a few years before they had a family, and travel as often as possible. They made it to New York and then Canada. While travelling through Canada Mel got food poisoning, only she never stopped vomiting and it was after being admitted to hospital for dehydration that they found out she was pregnant.

Carter ran into the house and and tried to make the house presentable. Twenty minutes, later Mel pulled onto the driveway and he exhaled the fear he had been feeling.

CHAPTER 14

—·—

MEL

Mel paused as she turned the engine off, wondering why she'd thought this might be a good idea, aware she was stepping out of the car regardless of her doubt.

'You came,' Carter said as he stood in the doorway, looking anxious.

'I did.' Mel looked away from him, embarrassed by the nervous energy that wrapped around her insides.

'I thought maybe I could fix us a drink and then we could sit outside,' Carter said.

'Good idea.' She smiled, feeling awkward at the formality of their conversation.

Mel scanned the room as she walked through the lounge towards the patio. There were definate signs that Carter was living here even though she suspected he'd tried his best to hide it. She could feel his eyes on her and her heart skipped. She froze and her face drained of colour.

'What? What is it?' Carter asked as he scanned her face and then the room. No words would come to her. Her eyes were fixated on the partially open briefcase with Ella's pink rag doll peeking out of it.

'Mel, I'm really sorry. I keep it in my brief case and well, I wasn't expecting you to come back here.' He quickly made his way to the briefcase and pushed the doll out of sight.

'You keep Ella's toy in your briefcase?' Mel asked, shocked. She longed to hold the toy.

'I know it's stupid, but I feel as if Ella's with me at work,' Carter said.

Again, Mel was taken back. 'All of this time I assumed you were handling things better than me and I guess to some degree I assumed you were moving on with your life.'

'How do you even do that? I didn't just lose a daughter, Mel. I lost a wife as well. I lost everything.'

Mel walked outside, carrying the weight of his words with her as she sat down and looked out at the lake. It was still a beautiful view in the light of day, even though it was tainted with dark memories now.

Carter sat next to her.

'I'm sorry,' she said. 'Our grief looked so different on the outside. I would look at you when I was crying, which was basically all the time, and I'd see you standing there looking strong. I shut you out. I thought you didn't understand.'

'We were both struggling, Mel. I didn't have the words to describe how I felt and there was part of me that did not feel entitled to grieve as intensely as you. You carried Ella for nine months and gave birth to her. I wasn't sure what the rule book allowed.'

'There is no rule book,' Mel said.

'I guess not.' Carter said, before turning to look at her. 'Do you think we can rewrite a new story? Would you be prepared to try?'

'I think so, but not here. Not in this house. It's too painful. Every time I look at the lake, I ask myself why I gave in and let her swim.'

'I know. It's bittersweet. Sometimes I love the memories this house holds, and I get comfort from seeing her things and being in her room, and other days I can't look at them because it's a stark reminder of what we lost, and it feels too overwhelming.'

'How should we do this?' Mel asked. 'We were married for years but in some ways, it feels like we are strangers now.'

'I think that's just because it ended so weirdly. We stopped communicating and we have to change that. We need to be honest with each other even if the truth might hurt. We have to find some way of getting through that because we were so good together, Mel, and we can be again.' Carter stood up and pulled her up by the hand and held her. It felt like coming home, the smell of him, the way she moulded into his arms and felt safe.

'How would you feel about counselling? Together, I mean,' Carter asked.

'I think I'd rather just see my own counsellor. I'm trying to imagine us sitting in a room talking about it all over again with someone new and I'm not sure how helpful that would be, to be honest.'

'I get it.' He looked her in the eye and the smell of his aftershave brought back so many memories.

'Is it okay if I kiss you?' he asked.

Mel's heart answered for her as his lips brushed hers and their mouths connected and heat travelled through her body, bringing her to life. It was as if a hunger had been released within them both as they clung to each other, their breath coming in short sharp bursts, their mouths unable to break free from one another. They stepped apart from each other, breathless, and walked inside the house, undressing each other in between kisses.

'My God, you have no idea how long I have wanted this,' Carter said as he traced her neck with kisses all the way down to her nipples. He sucked until she could feel every inch of her skin tingle with anticipation and then she pushed his head down and arched her back as his tongue made contact with the core of her. She moaned out loud and moved, she wanted to save the climax for when he was inside of her.

'I've missed the taste of you,' Carter said.

His words and eye contact were so intoxicating. She touched his penis and rhythmically moved him up and down before taking him in her mouth.

He pulled out of her mouth with a moan and lay her down, guiding his shaft into her. They clung together, breath ragged and hot as they created a dance of love and lust until they climaxed. Their shouts of pleasure reverberated around the room.

They lay silent, almost afraid to move in case it broke the spell.

'I love you,' Carter whispered.

'I know you do. I love you too,' Mel replied.

'Let's go away on holiday. Let's make new memories and get to know each other all over again.'

Mel laughed. 'I think we just did.'

'Well, I'd like to spend a whole week or more rediscovering your body, amongst other things.'

'Mmm, can't say I'd object to that,' Mel said, 'but I start my teacher training in two months, so we would have to make it soon.'

Carters' eyes lit up. 'Teacher training?' He nodded in agreement. 'That's a perfect choice for you. You'll be an amazing teacher. You were always so great with—'

'It's okay Carter, you can say her name,' Mel said as she squeezed his hand.

'You were always so great with Ella,' Carter said, kissing her lips. 'What do you say? Let's go away somewhere and you can choose where we go.'

'How about Italy? We never did make it there and that was on our list of countries to visit.'

'Italy it is,' Carter said before wrapping Mel in his arms.

CHAPTER 15

— · —

MEL

Mel watched her mum fussing over the table setting.

'Mum it's fine. This is Carter. He's been here a thousand times, you really need to relax.'

'I just want tonight to be lovely, darling. Ari's coming with Jay and, well, it will be the first time I've had both of my daughters *and* their partners here for a long time,' Grace said.

Mel laughed. 'You make it sound like such a big deal, Mum.'

'It is to me. All I've ever wanted is to see you both happy and we've all been through more than our share of heartache and challenges. For once it will be nice to just eat some food, have a glass of wine and toast to happy times.'

Mel walked to her mum and hugged her. 'You're the best. Did I ever tell you that?'

The doorbell rang.

Mel opened the door to Carter, who was pulling a suitcase and carrying a bouquet of tulips and lilies.

'Hi babe,' Mel said.

'Hey, beautiful.' Carter kissed her. 'Ah ah! Hands off, these flowers are for your mum, not you.'

'Oh wow, way to impress her and not me.' She jabbed him in the ribs.

'I'll make sure you are swept off your feet tomorrow in 'EEtaly' he said, with a terrible attempt at an accent.

'I'll hold you to it,' Mel said.

'Grace, how are you? You look fantastic,' Carter asked as he handed her th flowers.

'Oh, you always were charming,' she said, blushing slightly. 'It's good to see you, Carter. I've missed you.'

'What is the delicious smell?' he asked.

'Herby roast potatoes, lasagne, salad, and garlic bread. And tiramisu for dessert!'

'Very Italian!' He smiled and Mel felt as if no time had passed at all as she watched the two of them talk and laugh like old friends.

Grace looked teary eyed. 'I've really missed this. The laughter, the house full of life, the family time. It's just lovely having you all together.'

'Okay, that's enough wine, Mum,' Ari said with a smile. 'Time for us to leave soon anyway so we can drop the travellers off.'

Mel stood and hugged her mum. 'See you in two weeks, Mama. Love you.'

'Have a great time and stay safe, you two,' Grace said as she waved them off from the door.

Mel and Carter said their goodbyes to Ari and Jay at Edinburgh airport, and they checked in for their flight to Heathrow.

'Just think, this time tomorrow we will be in Naples.' Carter squeezed her hand and raised his plastic glass of beer. 'Cheers, babe.'

'Cheers,' Mel said as she sat back and smiled to herself. 'I have to say that gin and tonic doesn't taste the same in a plastic cup though.'

'Just wait until we are eating pasta and drinking wine in the city of love tomorrow.'

❦ ⸭ ❧

Mel entered the room first and inhaled the subtle aroma of jasmine. A blanket of lights flickered before her eyes through the expansive window as she looked at the city below. A bottle of champagne in an ice bucket waited on the slim black table; ice shifting in the bucket as if trying to find comfort and space.

'Oh wow. That's so nice of them.' Mel picked up the bottle impressed at the hotel's generosity.

Carter laughed. 'Was it you?' Mel asked.

'I thought it would be a nice romantic start to our holiday and I also remember that when you drink champagne you get quite horny.'

Mel blushed. 'Well, you had better open it, but I really want to make that flight tomorrow so only one glass, we have to be up early.'

'Here you go, madame.' Carter handed her a drink. 'I wouldn't worry about sleep though. I have a feeling we won't be getting much.' He kissed her and pushed the thin straps of her top off her shoulders and kissed along her collarbone, grazing her nipples with his thumb.

'I have a better idea. How about we drink this in bed. I'm feeling quite tired.' Mel feigned.

'I knew this holiday was a good idea.' Carter murmured as Mel undressed.

Mel took a quick sip of champagne as Carter slid under the bed sheet, pulled her towards him and wrapped his arms around her naked body.

CHAPTER 16

— · —

CARTER

They landed in Naples at nine thirty am. The sun was shining and stepping off the plane Carter swore he could smell pizza. He was transfixed as they taxied to the hotel. The streets were bustling with people and activity.

The hotel was small but classic Italian baroque architecture. The walls were white and plain, but that just made the parquet floor and ornate brown ceiling stand out even more. The ceiling was decorated with cornices and covings, and it was sectioned to show off twelve ceiling roses which seemed excessive, but it was somehow fitting to the design of the building.

'Wow this room is everything! I'm taking a picture to send to Mum and Ari. And Jade! She would love to stay here,' Mel said.

Carter opened the patio doors that led onto a small balcony with ornate black iron railings, and views out onto a row of shops, cafes, and restaurants.

'Wow indeed. And smell that coffee, come out here Mel.' Carter inhaled deeply, smiling both inside and out.

Mel joined him on the balcony and linked his arm as they both soaked in their surroundings. 'Okay, where to? Let's go exploring.' Her eyes were dancing with excitement.

'Well, the castle is a ten-minute walk from here. *Maschio Angioino.*'

Mel pushed him gently. 'You'd better not be doing that horrid Italian accent the whole time we are here.'

'Ti Amo.'

She rolled her eyes. 'What does that even mean?'

'I love you.' He pulled her back into the room and onto the bed. 'I can show you how much if you like.'

'That can wait. Come on, let's go and see this castle.'

He put his hand on his heart. 'Rejection is hard to take.' Mel laughed and then pulled him out of the door in a hurry to get outside and explore their surroundings.

The castle was packed with tourists which created a slow walk through due to some rooms having a limit of five people.

'Look at this Carter,' Mel said, transfixed.

Carter looked down at a glass floor with ruins beneath it.

'They're Roman ruins. Isn't that amazing and also a bit weird.'

'Weird how?' He asked.

'Well, we learnt all about the Romans at school and now we're standing here looking at broken cups they drank from. Those history lessons were just words, but being here and seeing things, it just makes it so real.'

After photographs from the rooftop, which took an age to walk up to because the lift was broken, they decided to wander the area to find a restaurant for later that evening.

They meandered the streets close to their hotel and booked a table at a restaurant that overlooked the seafront. They arrived at four thirty to watch the sun set at five pm. The smell of garlic hung thick in the air and the chatter of Italian echoed around them.

'It's so beautiful here. The sea looks like it's sprinkled with diamonds,' Mel said. Carter noticed how relaxed and happy she looked.

They talked until the restaurant closed and walked back to the hotel arm in arm, surprised at how many people were still out. The place felt alive, and the energy seemed to spread like a fast-rising tide, sweeping them along with it.

CHAPTER 17

— · —

MEL

Mel was no good at surprises and Carter had been teasing her since she woke at six am.

'Just tell me where we are going?' Mel asked.

'No, that's part of the fun. You look stunning by the way.' Carter took a photo of her as she stood in front of the patio doors wearing a beige Bardot style dress that hugged her body and fell just below the knee. In one hand she carried a small, jewelled bag, and in the other she held a glass of prosecco. She smiled her best smile as Carter took pictures from different angles.

'Can we at least go now?' Mel begged.

'Come with me, Mrs. Impatient,' he said as they exited their room.

Outside, the air was heavy with the smell of coffee beans and herbs. Vespas whizzed up and down the road and chatter from bars and restaurants bounced between the buildings. People were congregated in groups, sitting and standing. Laughter rang out, and Mel couldn't help but smile.

'I love it here.' She linked Carter's arm and her stomach danced in anticipation of the surprise ahead of her.

'Me too, and we're off to Rome tomorrow so more adventures await us.'

'It's so exciting.' She slipped her hand into his and they walked until they rounded a corner and she stopped in awe.

'Welcome to Teatro di San Carlo—the opera house,' Carter said.

Mel gasped. 'I've never been to the opera before.'

'Neither have I. Remember, we're rewriting the story, babe.'

The theatre's interior was extravagant red and gold. The ceiling was painted with cherubs and sunshine and clouds, in a mixture of light blues, white, and gold. It was breathtaking. They watched an opera which Mel could neither pronounce nor understand but it was a unique experience and one she would repeat in a heartbeat.

'What an end to an amazing few days in Naples. Thank you so much. You really thought of everything.'

Carter smiled at her. 'What's your tourist synopsis of Naples then?'

Mel scanned the scenery surrounding her and tipped her head to one side, trying to find the right words. 'It's a fusion of rugged beauty and extravagance.'

'*Bellissimo.* Now let's get back to the room and get that dress off, it looks rather tight.' Carter slipped his hand behind her neck, pulling her towards him.

This is how people lose themselves, Mel thought.

The Basilica looked like a grand palace as they stood before it. The traditional stone was offset by a huge blue and gold dome that sat atop. Inside, the marble columns and archways were adorned with carvings of angels and cherubs.

'It's hard to believe they started building this place in 1506,' said Mel. 'How did they manage it?''

'And it's still standing,' Carter said. 'We seem to struggle to build roads that last more than six months, let build alone something this magnificent.'

Rome was a blur. They took a trip to the Colosseum, which used to hold 65,000 spectators back in its day. They visited the Sistine Chapel, where they took dozens of photographs of Michelangelo's paintings. They ate suppli, a deep-fried breaded meat and mozzarella snack, and slices of pizza as they walked the streets taking photographs of buildings and people. They drank coffee in the mornings as they sat on metal chairs outside of cafés, watching the world unfold before them. Models doing photoshoots, tourists heaped up with backpacks, maps and cameras, people going to and from work. It was invigorating to be surrounded by so much activity.

They placed their luggage in the storage room after checking out and walked the short distance to the café that had become a favourite during their short stay.

'I don't think I've ever visited a place that felt so alive,' Mel said.

Carter sat back in his chair, having finished his croissant. 'So alive?'

'Look around you. There's a buzz in the air. The place is literally vibrating with energy. Think about holidays in Spain. They're great, but it's a different energy. Everyone is relaxed, winding down. Here, there's so much to see and do and maybe it's the history associated with the place, but it just feels magical somehow.'

'You're right. Speaking of which, we only have a few hours before we fly to Venice, so let's walk to the Trevi fountain and make a wish.'

The air was cool, the morning sun just starting to show itself as they approached the fountain and the hordes of people already gathered. The fountain stood 85ft tall and almost 65ft wide and featured a huge statue of Neptune, god of the sea, being pulled by two horses, one calm and the other unruly which was said to represent the unpredictability of the sea. Legend had it that if you threw a coin in the fountain, it would ensure a return to Rome. Mel looked to her left and a little girl about three years old was dancing next to her mum, her red dress twirling as she spun around, her dark hair in pigtails with red ribbons. She was transfixed.

Carter saw her staring at the girl. 'Hey,' he said gently, 'are you okay?'

'I'm fine,' she lied, before distracting him with conversation.

The following morning, Mel woke in Venice with memories clenched between her teeth.

'What is it?' Carter asked.

The tears rolled down her cheeks and sobs racked her body. Carter held her until she was calm enough to talk.

'Seeing that girl yesterday made me think of Ella, and then I was overwhelmed with the injustice of never being able to make more memories with her. I sometimes hate that other people have that. There're so many things I think of. I feel a sense of loss that we will never see her marry, maybe have children, a career, all of the things that other parents get to be a part of. It's just so wrong and there are times I feel so much anger because we are robbed of all of those special times.'

'I know baby. I know.'

Mel showered and tried to wash away her grief. Some days were like that; heavy and smothering, difficult to think about anything else. She was thankful to share that with Carter. She did her best to hide it, keep her grief private from others, but sometimes it spilled out in the form of words and behaviour. There are so many layers to grief that are invisible to the non grievers of this world. You envy your own family and friends because they have their child and you don't. You can envy the fact that they live a normal life without the heaviness and darkness of grief that resides in you every day. A constant reminder of what was. Mel closed her eyes and let the hot water carry away the tears.

❯❯ ·•◆•· ❮❮

They had prebooked a tour of Venice islands Murano, Burano, and Torcello. She tried to leave her mood ashore as she stepped onto the boat. She took pictures of the houses along the canal way, painted in bright greens, reds, blues, and yellows. They passed pristine bridges and churches in terracotta, and they walked along cobbled streets with the sun on their backs as they made their way to a glass factory. It was a welcome distraction.

That evening they ate dinner at Terazza Danieli, a rooftop restaurant overlooking the Adriatic Sea and city. The smell of the sea was heavy in the air, and Mel could taste salt on her lips.

When the waiter placed their food in front of them, she looked at Carter's order of sardines and pulled a face. 'I don't know how you can eat that stuff, it's so gross.'

'When in Rome, babe, or should I say Venice. You can't visit another country and not try their traditional dishes.'

'Risotto is Italian.'

'And boring, and in every restaurant in Scotland and England that sells pizza.'

'Well, I'd rather be boring than eat those.' She pointed her fork at his plate and laughed. She was aware of someone watching and she glanced up to see a woman on the table opposite smiling at her.

'Lovely evening,' the woman said cheerily.

'Yes, it is,' Mel replied.

'Are you here on honeymoon?'

'Erm, no.' Mel felt awkward and unsure of what to say.

'We've been married for almost five years,' Carter piped up.

'Oh lovely.' She smiled again. 'No children yet?'

Mel started choking on her risotto. Carter rushed around and patted her on the back and by the time she had composed herself the woman had lost interest.

'Are you okay?' said Carter.

'Well, I didn't need the Heimlich manoeuvre, so I guess so.'

'You know what I mean.'

'Let's just change the subject.' Mel was aware she was a little short with Carter.

'Fancy a walk when you've finished your food?'

Mel nodded, relieved to change the setting and avoid any potential conversations with strangers.

Black and grey clouds hung low as they walked along the canal way and took pictures next to the gondolas before the rain started. They made their way back to their accommodation by ducking in and out of shopfronts and doorways and then they sat on the balcony, watching the lighting break the clouds into silver fragments as thunder clapped the air. The weather felt quite fitting to Mel's mood.

Mel sat on top of her case so that she could coax the zip around its corner. She had bought too many mementos and she'd be surprised if she was not over her baggage allowance.

'I wish we could have stayed longer, Carter.'

'I think we'd be broke if we'd stayed any longer. It's been fabulous though, and I've loved every minute of us being alone, without distractions or interference.'

'I know. I didn't realise how much I needed to get away. It makes me reluctant to go back to normal life, although I am excited about the teacher training!'

'So how about we rent somewhere together until the house sells and then we can decide where to buy or build?'

'If you're sure that's what you want.'

'I think life has taught us both that there's no to-morrow guaranteed. We have no need to wait and quite frankly after spending every day with you, I'd find it impossible to let you go.' Carter wrapped his arms around her and Mel rested her head on his shoulder.

'This holiday was the best ever.' She managed to say before he silenced her with a kiss.

CHAPTER 18

— · —

MEL

The past eighteen months had been a blur of study, work, and house planning. The house in the Lakes had sold. After many discussions, they had bought a renovated farmhouse with an acre of land, just outside of Dunbar.

Mel smiled to herself and sat nervously, hands clasped on her lap, waiting on her name being called. She could feel eyes on her as she stood and made her way to the stage. She was aware of clapping as she took the scroll in her left hand. She was a newly qualified teacher and as she grasped hold of her degree, she could not remove the smile from her face. Carter, her mum, sister, and Jade were clapping, and her mum was having what she called a happy cry. They all hugged her and congratulated her. Her life was about to take on a new direction and she'd never felt more ready for the change.

Mel had been working in the school for six months prior to the school summer break as part of her placement and today was the first day of teaching her own year group. The children lined up outside with their parents, looking all shiny and new in their uniforms. She took a deep breath to calm her nerves and opened the door to greet them.

'Good morning class Five A. I am Mrs. Steadman.' She beamed at the row of children and parents in front of her. 'Please follow me to the classroom and hang your coats on the peg with your name.' She exhaled slowly. This was way more nerve wracking now that she was the one in charge with no one to rescue her.

The parents hovered, making sure their kids were fine. Some cried, some needed to tell her specifics about their child, worry evident on their faces, and others didn't blink an eye as they left. Somehow, she managed to get some sort of order in the room and the morning was over before she could blink an eye.

'How's it going with the new class? Any monkeys climbing the walls?' Jules asked at morning break. Jules taught in the classroom next door to Mel and the minute they had met, they had clicked. Jules had been teaching for three years and had been so supportive to Mel during her degree placement.

Mel smiled. 'A few with ants in pants but so far so good.'

'Well, I'm just next door so shout out if you need anything.'

The day passed in a blur. As Mel drove home, she was thankful it would still be light for a few hours yet. She took a lasagne out of the freezer and made a mental note to buy her mum some flowers. At least one night each week they ate courtesy of her mum's left overs. Her phone vibrated and danced on the bench top.

'Hi sis. How are you?' Mel asked as she answered her phone.

'I'm *very* well. Do you fancy meeting me for a coffee after work tomorrow?' Ari asked.

'Don't you know teachers survive on at least four coffees a day? Of course I'll meet you. Usual place?'

'Yeah. See you at four?'

The following day Ari was sitting at a table, glowing from head to toe. She had a summer dress on even though it was September and Mel wondered how she wasn't freezing. She was tanned and it suited her. Her blue eyes sparkled, and her dark blonde hair had a few highlights woven through, which added to her summer vibe.

'You're looking hot, sis. There's no need to glow this hard for me you know,' said Mel.

'I'm so excited I can barely sit still.'

'What's happening?' Mel asked. 'Why the excitement?'

Ari pushed a wrapped gift towards her.

'It's not my birthday. This is weird but thanks.'

'Open it. Quickly,' Ari said, clasping her hands together nervously before tapping her manicured nails on the table, impatiently.

'Jeez, give me a chance,' Mel said as she removed the ribbon and peeled off the white rosebud paper. She lifted the lid off the blue velvet box in front of her.

Ari urged her to keep going.

Mel unwrapped the white tissue. Before her was a Perspex heart with ribbon attached and the words: 'Will you be my bridesmaid?' She stared opened mouthed at her sister.

'Oh my God! Yes! Yes, I'll be your bridesmaid!' They hugged and squealed. 'Everyone's looking at us.'

Ari grinned. 'I really don't care.'

'Ring, show me the ring! I can't believe I didn't notice.' Mel grabbed her sister's hand and Ari revealed a square diamond. 'Oh wow, that's beautiful! Tell me about the proposal.'

'Jay took me to a hotel and when we ate dinner he popped back to the room. He had champagne delivered in an ice bucket and he'd scattered rose petals along the floor. There was more to it than that, but that's the gist of it. It was so romantic.'

'I'm really happy for you, Ari.' Mel hugged her.

'Thanks, Mel. We've got lots to look forward to. The wedding is in December.'

'December! Will you have time to plan a wedding in a few months? And it will be freezing.'

'It will be a quiet wedding, so not a lot to plan really and not many people marry at that time of year so it will be fine, I've already called a few places and there is availability. And we'll have a marvellous thing called central heating so no fear of freezing, sis.'

They talked weddings until cafe staff were gently ushering them outside so that they could lock up.

Once in her car Mel allowed the tears that she had kept hidden to flow. As happy as she was for her sister it was occasions like this that hit hard. While she knew time could not stand still, it broke her to think that he daughter would not be by her side on Ari's special day.

Chapter 19

Mel

Mel entered the bridal shop, which had an aroma of Chanel perfume and bank notes. She watched the bridal stylist fuss over Ari and rush around ensuring that everyone was settled and happy. Jay's mum and her mum sat on a pink velvet sofa sipping prosecco while Mel and Carla, Ari's other bridesmaid, sat opposite them on a white velvet sofa. There were three sofas in total and they were arranged in a semi-circle in front of the stage-come-catwalk, so that the bride could show off the dress.

'Ladies here you are,' said the glamorous assistant as she rounded the corner with a tray of nibbles. 'Once you've chosen the dress Ari, we will feast on macaroons and chocolate coated strawberries, but as a precaution we wait until after the dresses have been tried on.' The assistant's expression indicated that chocolate strawberries and wedding dresses did not mix.

'Totally understandable,' her Mum said is a slightly posh accent. She always acted a little different around people when she felt the need to impress them.

'Let's browse some dresses and you can tell me what styles you like, Ari. And remember we have our own dressmaker who will ensure that any dress fits you to perfection.' Clarissa the store owner said loudly as she ushered Mel's sister behind the white silk curtains.

The first one Ari modelled made her look like an extra for Cinderella. The second one was off the shoulder, fitted but not clinging to every skin cell and she walked out to gasps.

'Oh, darling that looks stunning on you.' Her mum beamed.

'I agree sis, that looks gorgeous on you.' Mel said.

'Lots more to try before she buys!' An enthusiastic Clarissa said. Mel guessed her to be in her late forties. Her nails were immaculate, hair shimmied into a neat bob and her brow was crease free. She had a figure she must have to work for, because she looked like she could model the gown herself.

'Dress number three!' Clarissa announced and Ari stepped forward. Mel was momentarily stunned. Her sister was wearing a white fitted corset with full skirt covered in tiny diamante.'

'Do a twirl.' Clarissa encouraged.

Ari turned revealing the back of her bodice which was laced with thick white ribbon.

Clarissa ran behind the curtain and returned with a taupe faux fur stole. She draped it around Ari's shoulders and fitted a diamante clasp in the centre. 'Well, what do you think ladies?' Clarissa asked with her arms outstretched towards the glowing bride to be.

Ari's eyes searched out Mel and Grace. 'Well?' She asked, with a smile.

Mel turned to see tears flowing from her mum's eyes and broad smile fixed on her face.

'That's the dress.' Mel said.

'My darling, you are beautiful.' Grace gushed.

'I totally agree.' Jay's mum and Carla said in unison.

Ari wiped a tear from her eye and nodded to her mum.

'How much is it?' Ari asked Clarissa.

'Two thousand seven hundred pounds for the dress and stole. Go and chat with your mum and we'll bring out some champagne.'

'The dress is just beautiful, darling.' Grace wiped her eyes with a cotton tissue and Mel wondered where she'd magicked that from because she's never seen her mum with a cotton tissue, ever.

'The dress is almost three thousand pounds mum,' Ari whispered out of Clarissa's earshot.

'Darling, I said I would pay for your dress so stop worrying. It's fine.'

'Are you sure, Mum? I feel like—'

'Your sister had money spent on her for her wedding and you will get the same amount too. And if that is the dress you want, we will buy it today.'

'You have to buy that dress sis. It's perfect!' Mel hugged Ari.

Ari hugged her back and then did another twirl. 'Someone pour the champagne and bring out those nibbles. I've found my dress!'

CHAPTER 20

— · —

GRACE

Ari's wedding was in a hotel with its own chapel. It was a small intimate affair, with only thirty people in total. Grace stood in front of her daughter, speechless, taking in the vision before her. Ari's hair was piled on top of her head with some loose curls tumbling down and a tiara nestled between a row of curls, only showing itself in a certain light. Ari wore the fur stole and carried a bouquet of blushing beige roses and white geraniums. A tear fell from her eye as she looked at her daughter.

'You look so beautiful. I wish your father could be here to see you,' Grace said.

'He's with us in spirit, Mum, I can feel it.' Ari grasped her hand and swallowed down her emotion.

'Let's go, then,' Grace said as she linked her arm through Ari's and walked towards the stone staircase where Mel and Carla were waiting. 'Girls, you look stunning.' Grace gave them both a hug. 'You can go ahead of us, and Ari and I will follow you down once you get to the bottom.'

The music started and the girls walked down in unison in their taupe silk dresses and white stoles. The colour theme even managed to blend in with the chapel surroundings and stonework.

Grace could hear the gasps as they transcended the stairs and people caught sight of the bride. She had never felt so proud. Ari took her place next to Jay and Grace took her seat.

'She looks absolutely beautiful,' Karen said as she squeezed Grace's hand. 'I know you miss Tom and today must be hard for you, but he would be so proud and not just of the girls, he would be proud of you too.'

'Stop, or I'll be a blubbering mess and all this make-up will smudge and make me look horrendous.' They smiled at each other and then turned their attention to the bride and groom, who were just about to start their vows.

After photographs, they made their way into the conservatory. The scene was out of this world. The ceiling had been draped with white fabric that twinkled with lights. The tables were dressed in white brown and golds, and gold lanterns were placed on the floor next to the windows. Outside there was a marquee with bar and photo booth. It was the perfect mixture of elegance and fun.

Grace sat quietly reminiscing about her own wedding day, which had been in a registry office. Simple, cost effective and no fuss, that's what she had wanted. Things were so different now, although aside from the dress this wedding was far less fancy than some she had been to.

'Are you okay, Grace?' Karen asked.

'Yes honey, thanks. I was just thinking back to mine and Tom's wedding day and thinking how different things are now. I would have given anything for him to be here today.'

'I know you would.'

Grace checked herself. 'Enough of my maudlin. There are enough days in the year for me to find another one to spend reminiscing. Today I intend to enjoy myself and just look at the bride and groom. They look so happy.'

'Never mind them, look at Mel and Carter,' Karen said, smiling.

'He couldn't take his eyes off her earlier. It's so sweet and I'm so happy that they've come through it all.' Grace said.

The best man tapped his glass, and everyone hushed as he launched into his speech.

It was a day that brought Grace a mixture of love, joy, and sadness. She really felt lonely with couples surrounding her and it made her wonder whether she should do as the girls suggested and find herself someone to spend time with. Thoughts for another day perhaps.

CHAPTER 21

— · —

ARI

Ari knocked and walked into the house with her wedding album balanced in one arm. It had taken eight weeks to get copies of the pictures and she couldn't wait to show them off. She saw her mum standing in front of the mirror, putting lipstick on.

'Oh, I should have called. I brought the wedding photos to show you. Are you going out?' Ari watched her mum grab her bag and she could swear she was blushing. 'Are you okay?'

'Yes, yes, I just wasn't expecting you and I'll be late if I look at the pictures now, darling. I do feel so awful saying that, it sounds like I'm not interested,' Grace said.

'Don't be silly, we can come over later tonight if you like. Where you off to, anyway?' Ari asked, thinking her mum seemed a bit flustered.

'Oh, just to lunch,' Grace said dismissively.

'Are you blushing, Mum?'

'Stop it, Ari. I'm just going for lunch that's all.'

'With a man?' Ari gasped.

'Well, haven't you and your sister been telling me to do this for long enough?' Grace said.

'Oh my Lord, does Mel know?'

'I'm sure she soon will.' Grace shook her head, as if trying to shrug off Ari's interest.

'Look, it's nothing to get excited about. It's only John from the fundraiser group. I've known him for years and I'm sure it's not exactly a date.'

'Oh no, this is wonderful news,' Ari grinned, wide eyed. 'You should invite him to dinner one evening and we can meet him.'

'Don't be silly, and please stop making a big deal of this. I have to go darling, come by later and I'd love to see the photos when I'm not in a rush. Can I leave you to lock up?'

'Sure,' Ari said, taking her phone out of her pocket to call Mel.

Later that evening, Ari arrived at her mum's with Mel so they could all look through the photographs.

'I love them all! I'm finding it so hard to choose just one,' Grace said.

'Same,' said Mel. 'But I do like this one of the three of us, what do you think, Mum?'

'Oh, that's lovely, darling. I can't decide between that one and the one of Ari and Jay at the altar, so I think I'm going to get both to frame, and I'll have my own mini album as well.'

'I'll have number three for a framed picture and same as Mum, a smaller album with them all,' Mel said.

'Don't you want one of you and Carter, honey? This one is beautiful. Look at the way he looks at you.'

Mel blushed. 'Can you not, Mum?'

'It's a blessing when a man looks at you that way after you've been together for years.'

'Speaking about men,' Ari said, 'how was your date?'

'Yes, how was your date, Mum?' Mel looked at Ari and they burst out laughing.

'Wow, you two are still like kids at times, and I told you it wasn't a date,' Grace said quietly but firmly.

'Touchy.'

'It was definitely a date,' Ari said, nodding to Mel. 'Too touchy for it not to be.'

'Oh, for goodness' sake. Okay, so we had lunch. It was nice and I've known John for a long time now, and yes, he has asked me out again.'

Mel stood up and hugged her mum. 'I'm only winding you up. I'm actually really happy that you have found someone.'

'Me too,' Ari added.

'It's only early days. We're just hanging out and enjoying each other's company, that's all. So don't get carried away, you two.'

'All the same, it would be nice to meet him sometime,' said Ari. 'Maybe Jay and I will have a barbecue, and you could invite him along.'

'Don't you think it's a bit early for that?' Grace asked.

'If you'd just met him, I'd say yes, but you've known him for years, so it will be fine.'

Grace's brow creased in concern. 'Let me know when that's happening, and I'll think about it. But what if he doesn't want to go? He might think it's too soon, or worse, he might think I'm desperate.'

'Of course he'll want to go. He's keen on you, or he wouldn't have asked you out,' Ari said.

'Oh, you kids are so confident these days,' Grace said.

'That's settled, then. We will meet John at the barbecue,' Ari said.

Mel laughed as her mum walked into the kitchen wearing her 'I give up' face, then returned with a plate of warm cheese scones.

CHAPTER 22

— · —

GRACE

Grace felt like a teenager again, nervous at the thought of inviting a man to meet her parents. Only this time it was not the parents he would be meeting; it was her daughters and sons-in-law.

Grace parked the car and smiled as John was waiting at the gate.

'Hello. You look lovely as always,' he said as he sat in the passenger seat.

Grace flushed slightly. 'Thanks, John. You look nice too.' She found it awkward giving out compliments to someone other than Tom. She'd also found it hard to find the balance between making an effort and not being too over the top. She didn't want to look desperate.

'How's your week been?' John asked.

'Quiet. The family came over for dinner last night but aside from that and a coffee with Karen, I've not done a lot. What about you, John?'

'Pottered in the garden between the rain and I went fell walking with Macca yesterday. I tell you what, he might be sixty-eight but that man is as fit as a fiddle. He put me to shame and I'm five years younger.'

Grace smiled. 'That sounds nice—and exhausting.'

She parked her car and they walked the short distance to her favourite restaurant. They had just sat down when a waitress appeared out of nowhere just as Grace was about to mention the barbecue. *Damn it,* she thought to herself. *Why am I so nervous?*

'Can I take your order?' the young girl asked, pen at the ready.

Grace had barely looked at the menu and now felt pressured, so she scanned it quickly. 'I'll have a beetroot and feta salad please, and a spritzer. Thanks.'

As soon as the girl walked away, she mentally scolded herself for ordering a meal with beetroot when she was wearing white.

'Ari is having a barbecue in a week or two and she extended the invite to you. If you want to come of course, but no pressure.' Grace spoke too quickly and waited for him to reply, and then felt annoyed at herself for allowing the girls to coax her into this. It was too soon.

'I'd love to.' John smiled. 'I've heard so much about the girls I feel as if I already know them.'

'Oh, you would? That's great. I'll let her know.'

'Don't sound so surprised, Grace. I've been asking you out to dinner for at least a year. We're too young to play hard to get and I wear my heart on my sleeve.'

Grace felt her face redden and she also felt a mixture of emotions. 'I know, it's just that I don't want to give you the wrong impression. I'm not sure that I'm ready for anything...' She struggled to find the word.

'Grace, look at me. I have my own house, you have yours. I'm not about to propose to you, but I would like to be in a relationship with you. Don't overthink it, we'll just let things take their natural course.'

Grace smiled and felt herself relax. 'You have to understand this is so foreign to me. The last time I dated, I was sixteen years old. That was forty years ago, John.'

'Well, I'm not exactly an expert myself, but I think we're doing okay, don't you?'

'If I manage to eat this salad without getting beet-root all over this shirt, we're doing great!'

John stood on the driveway. Grace could tell some-thing was up and wondered if he was having second thoughts.

'What is it, John? Have you changed your mind?'

'No, not at all. Believe it or not, I'm a little nervous, Grace.'

'You've nothing to be nervous about,' she reassured him.

'That's easy for you to say. What if they don't take to me?'

'Now who's overthinking things?' Grace laughed. 'Come on, let's go.'

Ari's house was a Victorian terrace which was like a Tardis once you were inside. The garden was large and private, and that was what had sold it. That, and the four bedrooms plus attic. Grace suspected they might be planning a large family.

'Mum.' Ari hugged her.

'Hello, darling.' Grace whispered in her ear: 'Please behave.'

'You must be John.' Ari extended her hand. 'It's so nice to meet you.'

'Lovely to meet you as well, thanks for the invite.'

'Come through to the garden,' Ari said as she led the way. 'Can you believe the sun is shining? Mel and Carter are on their way, they just stopped off for some drinks and snacks.'

'What's cooking?' Grace asked. 'It smells delicious.'

Ari pointed to Jay. 'This chef over there has chicken on the rotisserie, marinated beef kebabs and lamb koftas cooking on the charcoal.'

Jay looked slightly embarrassed. 'You can't spring it on me that we're hosting a barbecue and then tell me I'm chef when I've only used the bloody thing once.' He pointed at the barbeque. 'A man has to practice until he can perfect something, right John? Can't be poisoning our guests.'

'Let's just say I've ate a lot of kebabs,' Ari teased.

Grace turned to John. 'At least you weren't the only one nervous,' she whispered and smiled.

'Hi!' a voice called out from behind them, and Mel appeared with her arms full of bags. She placed them on a chair. 'Wine, crisps, nuts, and chocolate. What more could we want, aside from good company? Speaking of which, hi John, it's lovely to meet you.'

Jay started serving up food before reloading the barbeque.

'This is a feast and a half,' Ari said, looking at the table laden with food. 'You boys will be sorted for work lunches for a few days, by the look of it. I can't believe you're putting more food on, Jay.'

'Better to have too much than not enough,' he said as he flipped burgers.

'You have a lovely family Grace, you're very lucky to have two daughters who get along well, plus two smashing sons in-law. Me and Sal weren't blessed with kids, and I always imagined family time a little something like this.'

Grace reached for his hand. 'Thank you, John, that means a lot to hear you say that. I am lucky. The only thing that was missing was company and I've found that now.'

'Watch out guys,' said Ari, 'the oldies are getting loose on the wine, and they've just held hands!'

Grace threw a napkin at Ari, and they all started laughing and Grace felt the happiest that she had in a long time.

CHAPTER 23

—·—

GRACE

Grace lit the candles and placed the cutlery next to the placemats. A waft of jasmine and sandalwood filled the air, carrying a feeling of peace and contentment.

'Mum, are you sure this is the right way to do things?' Ari asked, as she chewed on her bottom lip.

'I think regardless of how it's done darling, it will always be a tenuous situation.'

'It feels a little wrong this way. Maybe I should just speak to Mel on my own.'

'Darling, relax. It will be fine, and stress isn't good for you.'

Jay wrapped his arms around Ari from behind. 'Your mum's right. Relax, babe. Look, I know things were hard when it all happened, but this is something to celebrate, not hide from.'

Mel entered the house and slumped on the sofa. 'Carter's just parking the car. God, what a day, my head is banging. Some kids could talk the leg off a table.' She rubbed her temples and closed her eyes.

Grace exchanged looks with Ari, then turned to Mel. 'Hello darling, come and give your old mum a hug.'

'You're not old, Mum.' Mel hugged her and kissed her on the cheek.

'I brought wine,' Carter sang out as he entered the room. He placed the wine on the kitchen bench and seemed oblivious to the lack of response from Ari or Jay. 'What delights have you cooked for us tonight, Grace?'

'Nothing too fancy. You've got a choice of beef bourguignon or chicken chasseur.'

'Noice. Where's John?' Carter asked.

'I didn't ask him, I thought we could just have some family time the five of us,' Grace said.

'Don't say the romance of the century is over,' Mel said in mock horror.

Grace swatted her with a tea towel. 'How about you mind your business and go and sit, because I'm about to serve food.'

Grace set the casserole dishes down and took a seat, her stomach tense with the impending conversation.

'Dive in, everyone.' She savoured moments like this, when it felt as if time stopped while everyone alternated between silent eating, flurried chatter, and occasional laughter.

Carter rubbed his stomach and let out a sigh of satisfaction. 'That was so good. I wish you'd consider my offer, Grace.'

'What offer's that?' she asked with raised eyebrows.

'To be our live-in chef.'

'While we're all in good spirits, there's something we need to say.' Everyone turned to Ari and Jay. 'We weren't sure how to do this, but well there's something we wanted to tell you.' She paused, looking unsure, and Grace could feel her nerves. 'We're pregnant!' She said quickly and glanced at Mel.

Grace looked at Carter and Mel. Carter's face lit up and he offered congratulations. Mel, on the other hand, she looked like someone had just knocked the wind out of her. She congratulated them both, but she was upset. No one else seemed to have noticed, but a mother could read her child like a book.

'Are you okay, Mel?' she asked as they stood in the kitchen drying dishes a short while later.

'I'm fine,' she said a little too brightly.

'This is your mother you're talking to. I know you better than you think. You're probably shocked, and I imagine you have a lot of emotion swirling around your head right now. Your sister really wasn't sure how to go about this, so don't be too hard on her.'

'Are you sure you're not a witch? You seem to be able to read my mind.'

'You're still processing the news, but this is a happy time for your sister and Jay.'

'It's not that I'm not happy for her, Mum. For them. It's just...'

'I know darling. I know.' She hugged her daughter and hoped that Mel would see this for the blessing that it was.

CHAPTER 24

— · —

MEL

Mel walked into the staff room and plonked herself down in a chair. It was eight am and there were three teachers chatting in a huddle, one or two in classrooms and one regular would rock up at the last minute like she did every day, no doubt. The staff room had a distinct smell: food, books, exhaustion. Not that one could smell exhaustion, but it certainly hung in the air.

'What's up with you?' Jules asked as she sat down next to her.

'Oh, nothing.' She could feel Jules's eyes on her. 'Stop staring at me, it's weird.'

'I'll stop staring when you start talking.'

'Okay, but not here. The walls have ears.' She flicked her eyes to Dawn, who had just walked through the door. Dawn was the kind of teacher the kids disliked as well as the parents. She spent her days gossiping about the children and putting down the parents, and she seemed to get some sort of buzz from it. The first time Mel had met her, Dawn had eyed her from head to toe, and because Mel refused to join in with her toxic gossiping, Dawn had made it clear she did not like her. If she thought there was a sniff of gossip though, she was like a fly on shit.

They went to the safety of Jules's classroom. 'Okay spill, Mrs Steadman. What's up?' Jules asked.

'Look, it's nothing,' Mel said and Jules raised her eyebrows. 'It's just that last night my sister announced she's pregnant and I guess I just feel a bit weird about it.'

'Oh. And there's you saying it's nothing.'

'I feel bad. I mean, they're married and it's what most couples do, have a family, so it's not a surprise. Yet there I was, surprised! I felt as if someone had taken the floor from beneath me and I did my best to fake my happiness. My mum saw straight through it, though.'

'It must have brought up a lot of memories and that couldn't have been easy,' Jules said gently.

'That's exactly what mum said.'

'How do you feel today, now you've had some time to process it?'

'Still processing, I think. I feel confused. I'm happy and excited for them but also dreading the baby arriving. Does that sound bad?'

'I'd use the word understandable rather than bad, Mel.'

'The thought of going to Mum's and seeing a baby… I just feel so torn. I barely slept last night for having dreams about Ella.'

'It must be hard for you, but by the time the baby is due to arrive I'm sure you will be just as excited as everyone else.'

'Maybe,' Mel said. Dawn swung around the door-frame, causing them both to jump. 'Oh, hi ladies, I just wondered if you'd seen Brett around?'

'No, we haven't seen him,' Mel said, feeling annoyed with her.

'Okay. Well, thanks anyway,' Dawn said as she walked off.

'Nosy bitch,' Jules said. 'She's probably been ear-wigging at that door since we left the staff room. God, I can't stand her.'

'Thanks, Jules.'

'What for? Calling Dawn a nosy bitch? She is one.'

'Thanks for understanding.'

'No need to thank me. Catch you at lunch?'

"I'm on duty, lucky me.' Mel smiled.

'Well, have fun with your little munchkins and I'll see you later this afternoon. You sure you're okay?'

'Yeah, I am, thanks.'

Mel sat at her desk, deep in thought. She was surrounded by children every day at work, yet her own sister having a baby evoked so many emotions in her. She didn't have time to think about it for long though, because a hoard of energetic kids ran along the corridor and waited noisily outside of the classroom.

She pushed aside her feelings and stepped into her role as teacher. 'Morning, class.'

'Morning Miss,' Cassie said.

Mel was momentarily stunned. Cassie was a new child in her class, and she looked so like Ella at times. 'Oh, hi Cassie. How are you this morning?' Mel asked.

'I'm well, thank you Miss. How are you?'

Mel chuckled to herself. She'd never met anyone quite like Cassie. She was so old fashioned in some ways, yet so full of life. She was like a little ray of sunshine when she walked into the classroom. All the kids were lovely in their own way, but it was special ones like Cassie who made her job bearable on the challenging days.

CHAPTER 25

— · —

CARTER

This was the second week in a row that Mel had talked nonstop about the little girl in her class. Carter watched her face glow when she talked about this child: *Cassie this, Cassie that, the outfit she wore yesterday, the way she sounded out a new word, and how she comforted another child in the class who was upset.*

'What about all the other kids in your class, Mel? Or is there just Cassie?' Carter asked, eyebrows raised. He didn't understand her fascination with this kid.

Mel stopped and looked at him, slightly stunned. He watched her swallow down whatever it was he'd triggered.

'Sorry,' she retorted. 'Stupid of me to think you'd be interested in my work!' She walked off into the kitchen and he followed her.

'Mel.'

She ignored him.

'Mel!' Carter said a little louder. 'Can you stop long enough for me to speak, please?'

She stopped, but had her back to him.

He walked around her to face her. 'Just to be clear, I *am* interested in your work, and you know I am. I just noticed you talk about Cassie a lot, and the fact that you're being so reactive says something.'

She opened her mouth to speak, but instead turned around and walked back into the kitchen.

'Let's not do this, Mel. This doesn't have to be something we fight about,' Carter said.

'Well maybe if you weren't so nasty, I would want to be in the same room as you.'

'Tell me what's going on here?' Carter asked. 'You come home every day talking about one child out of a class of how many? Twenty-four? I point that out to you and then you're angry with me. Why? Have I touched on something?'

'You're overreacting and making a mountain out of a molehill. She's cute and smart and she remin—'

'She reminds you of Ella.'

Mel pulled from him, tears pooling in her eyes. 'That's not what I was going to say,' she snapped, knowing full well that he was right. She grabbed her bag and walked out of the house.

He let her go. He hoped that by the time she came in from work, she might be willing to talk about it. They had recently talked about having another child and Mel wanted a baby, but the fear of something going wrong overshadowed her longing. They had started the process of registration with the fostering agency but deep-down Carter hoped she would change her mind and come around to the idea of them having another child of their own. They had attended grief counselling relating to Ella as part of the process, and he had thought that Mel was starting to heal but this thing with Cassie had thrown him. He wondered if Ari's pregnancy played a part in Mel's fascination with Cassie, because she'd not been the same since they had announced their pregnancy.

Over the next few months, Mel never mentioned Cassie again. She seemed busier at work, coming home later some evenings, but in general she was happier and seemed more at peace with the thought of being an aunty. They had completed the fostering process but had agreed to wait until after they had travelled during the next school break before bringing a child into their home.

Carter walked out of work and loosened his tie. He'd spent all week trying to find a loophole in the company policy so he could fire someone without the company being done for unfair dismissal. It was mind numbing but high pressured because if he fucked up, it lay on his shoulders. He was looking forward to a cold beer and a pizza in front of the TV, and with a bit of luck he would stay awake long enough to watch the footy.

Carter heard laughter as soon as he opened the door. He stopped in the hallway put down his briefcase, and walked to the lounge. Mel was sitting on the floor with a girl who had dark hair that fell to her shoulders, and for a second it took his breath away.

He grabbed hold of the door frame to steady himself. 'Ella,' he whispered to himself.

The girl turned and he wondered if she'd heard him. 'Who's that, Miss?' she asked Mel.

Mel turned, surprised to find him there watching them. She looked nervous. 'Cassie, this is my husband, Carter... Carter, this is Cassie.'

Carter was rendered speechless, and he stood rooted to the spot staring at the two of them as his brain tried and failed to process why there was a child in his house.

'Cassie's mum is unwell, and they don't have any family here. The hospital called the school because it was a sudden and unexpected situation so I said Cassie could come home with me and stay with us for a few days. I know that's not how things usually happen with the care system, but given that we are approved foster carers I thought it would be a good opportunity for us to dip our toes in the water.' Mel pushed the words out quickly as if wanting to be rid of them. She smiled awkwardly, waiting on his response.

The little girl stood up and brushed down her pinafore dress before walking towards him. She stopped and looked at the floor, before lifting her head shyly. 'Nice to meet you, Mr Carter,' she said, looking at him from under dark lashes.

Carter instinctively shook her hand, taken back by her charisma. 'Nice to meet you too, Cassie.'

He could see Mel beaming like a proud parent. His heart skipped a beat and he was unsure if it was because the girl in front of him looked so like his daughter that it felt like a cruel twist of fate, or whether it was because he saw something in Mel that couldn't be reined in.

'I'll leave you two to play your game.' He walked into the kitchen and opened the back door, gripping the door frame while breathing in the cool air. It felt like he had one foot in the past and another in someone else's life. Everything felt upside down.

In the living room, Mel asked Cassie to watch TV for five minutes while she prepared a snack. He snatched a beer from the fridge and savoured the cold liquid as it hit the back of his throat. Suddenly, he felt the urge to get shit faced.

Mel walked in, both hands up in front of her as if trying to halt any conversation before it began. 'Before you say anything, I know this is weird, but Cassie's mum went for a scan and they found a tumour. She is now in hospital waiting on an operation to remove it.

They are fairly new to the area and have no family that Cassie could stay with, so I did what I thought was a good deed.' She pleaded with him to understand.

He wanted to understand, he really did, but this felt wrong.. If the child had looked less like their daughter, he might have felt differently. Carter paced the floor of the kitchen, the tiles cool beneath his socks. 'I'm not happy about this, Mel.'

'What do you propose I do? Send her into care? Do you have any idea how anxiety provoking and disruptive that can be?' Mel said in a low whisper.

'How many teachers take their pupils home to live with them?'

'It's temporary, she's not come to live with us. This is not a normal situation, Cater.'

'You're telling me it;s not normal! And could she look any more like Ella? Jesus, Mel, I thought I was seeing a ghost when I walked in.'

Her eyes misted. 'I know, the resemblance is uncanny.'

'That's what worries me. You're too close to this kid. She's not yours and yet here you are inviting her into our house to live with us, without so much as a phone call with me to check that I'm okay with it.'

Mel put her head down. 'I admit that I should have called you and I'm sorry, babe,' Mel said. 'Things just happened so quickly, and I was really put on the spot. I had to come here with the social worker so she could check we had adequate room and that the house was suitable and then I had all this paperwork to sign.' She breathlessly explained herself, and he could barely think straight.

His life had just become alarmingly complicated, and nothing was stable or solid anymore. 'How many days?'

'Hopefully no longer than six, but it depends upon her mum's recovery.'

'Well, I guess there's not a lot we can do, but please don't expect me to play *Happy Families*, Mel. This is a weird as fuck situation. I feel as if I've walked into the wrong house.'

Mel wrapped her arms around him and kissed him on the cheek. 'It's temporary, babe. It will be fine, I'll see to everything so you've got nothing to worry about.'

It was eleven pm before Mel got into bed after checking Cassie for the hundredth time. Frankly, it was already driving him mad.

'Are you awake?' she whispered.

'I am now.'

'I just wanted to make sure she was okay. I can't imagine how strange this must be for her, being away from her mum and not knowing when she will see her next.'

'Yeah,' was all he could muster.

'You know what she said to me when I put her into bed?'

'I'd rather not, Mel. I'm pretty tired and still coming to terms with the fact I have a strange child sleeping in my house.'

'Okay. Good night and thanks for at least trying to understand. I know this is hard for you.'

The following morning, Carter watched them together. Mel had fallen back into the routine of being responsible for someone with an ease that intimidated him. She served up toast, cereal, and fruit for the three of them. A cup of orange juice was placed in front of Cassie. Reminders to wash hands and brush teeth punctuated the free-flowing conversation.

'I have to go into the office early, so I'll eat as I drive,' he said, as he grabbed a slice of toast and finished his coffee. As much as he was trying, he could not bring himself to sit at the table and do this thing with Cassie. He was aware of Mel looking at him, analysing and pretending she was okay with this. He felt bad for this little kid, he really did, but he also wished she was somewhere else.

'Oh, no problem,' Mel said, disappointment in her voice, and this was a red flag for him. Why was she so insistent on acting like this was completely normal?

'See you at dinner,' she shouted after him as he left the house.

Before he drove off, he scrolled through his phone contacts and hit dial as he hit the accelerator, making sure he was on the road so Mel could not hear the conversation he was about to have.

'Grace, good morning. How is my favourite mother-in-law?'

'Only you could say that and get away with it. Is everything okay, Carter? It's not like you to call me this early. Come to think of it, it's not like you to call me at all. What's up?'

'I wondered if you'd spoken to Mel yesterday.'

'No, why? Is everything okay?'

'Yes. No. Oh hell, I don't know.' After telling Grace about Cassie, he waited on her response.

'Well—' Grace paused as if trying to think what to say, 'it does sound a very unique situation and by the sound of it there were not a lot of options.' She swallowed down her doubts. 'Is it possible you're reading too much into it? I don't mean that to sound dismissive, I know it must be hard having a girl in the house, especially a one that looks so similar to Ella.'

'Maybe I am. Would you do me a favour and call around after Mel finishes work, see with your own eyes? That will at least put my mind at ease. I'm just worried she's become too attached to this kid.'

'Of course I will, and I'll call you afterwards if there's anything to worry about.'

Carter felt himself relax a little and hoped that Grace would be able to put his mind at ease. After all, it was only for a few days and maybe she was right. Maybe he was overthinking it.

CHAPTER 26

GRACE

Grace knocked on the front door and opened it. 'Just me.'

No response. She walked through to the kitchen and the smell of popcorn hit her, followed by squeals of laughter from the garden. Grace looked through the kitchen window and felt her breath leave her body. Mel was chasing a little girl around the garden and from the back this child was the image of Ella. It was unnerving and Grace understood why Carter had been so shaken. She felt frozen to the spot, watching her daughter and this girl in their own little world. She'd not seen Mel this alive since Ella had died.

'Oh Mum, hi!' Mel shouted and waved from outside. 'Come on, Cassie you can come and meet my mum.'

'Hello, darling.' Grace reached out and hugged her daughter. 'And who do we have here?' She looked at the child, feeling unsteady on her feet.

The child smiled at her and curtsied. 'Pleased to meet you, Miss. Do I call you Miss or something else?

'You can call her Grace,' Mel whispered in Cassie's ear.

'My name is Cassie, and my mum is in hospital because she's sick, so I am staying with Miss at her house. We've just had popcorn and we fed some to the birds.' She giggled and pulled gently on Mel's skirt. 'Come on, let's do it again. Please, Miss?'

Mel ran outside and Cassie followed. She shouted to the birds to come down and get some food and they proceeded to throw popcorn on the grass. Cassie was in kinks of laughter as seagulls and starlings descended on the grass to pick up their winnings before taking off again. Grace looked at her daughter and felt her stomach sink.

'Fancy a coffee, Mum? Mel asked as she skipped back into the house.

Grace nodded.

'Cassie, maybe you could put the TV on while I speak to my mum. We're just in the kitchen if you need anything. Okay?'

The child nodded obediently and sat herself on the sofa watching Peppa Pig.

Grace picked up her coffee and inhaled the aroma rather than look at Mel. 'So, you've managed to bring one of your pupils home with you. I must say I'm surprised.'

'I know, I was surprised too. It all happened so quickly, but she's such a delight to have around, I really don't mind.' Mel smiled, fondly looking through to the lounge.

'How long is she here for?'

Mel pulled a face. 'Well, initially I thought around five days, but they called to say her mum is going to be in hospital for at least another week and then her recovery could be a month or so.'

'And Carter supports this?' Grace asked a little too quickly.

'I wouldn't say supports it.'

'Well, it's important he does, and it's important that you listen to his views.' She took a drink. 'Can I be honest?'

'You usually are.' Grace recognised that look.

'I'm not sure this is a good idea, Mel. I was shocked when I first saw the girl.'

'Her name is Cassie,' Mel said, challenging Grace with her eye contact.

Grace patiently corrected herself. 'I was shocked when I first saw Cassie. It was like looking at Ella. I worry you are reliving the past through this girl, darling.' Mel stayed silent and Grace knew she was aware of it too. 'Have you thought about how this will affect you teaching her when she's living at your house? And afterwards?'

'It's temporary,' was all Mel would say.

'Is this—is this a reaction to your sister having a baby?'

'My God, not you as well!' Her voice was hushed but firm. 'This has nothing to do with Ari. Nothing at all.'

A small voice spoke up from the doorway: 'My tummy's hungry.'

'Oh gosh, I didn't realise the time, Cassie. How about I make your tea now and you can sit here and watch me.'

'Thank you!' Cassie replied, soaking up the attention.

Mel lifted her onto a chair and looked at Grace, face beaming in pride. There were silent words floating between them. *Look at her, Mum. See how good she is?*

Grace stood up. 'I have to go, darling, but I'll see you soon.' She hugged Mel, grabbed her bag and walked to the door.

'Say goodbye to Cassie, Mum!' Mel said indignantly.

Grace stopped, not turning around, and took several deep breaths. 'Bye, Cassie.'

It looked like rain outside. Grace sat in her car, heart beating too fast. Carter had been right to call her. Mel was far too attached to this girl. Grace dialled his number and drove. Carter answered.

'You were right, Carter. You are right. This is not healthy, this thing she has with that girl.'

'What do I do Grace?' he asked.

'I can't tell you how to fix this Carter, but maybe you could start by talking to her and telling her how you feel.'

'How do you propose I do that when she won't listen? She brought Cassie into our home without even asking me.'

Grace could hear the hurt in his voice. 'Make her listen. I never want her going back to that dark place she went to after Ella died. What happens when this girl needs to go back home? It doesn't bear thinking of, Carter. Do whatever you must to put an end to this.'

CHAPTER 27

— · —

MEL

Cassie had been with them five days now. Mel set her alarm a little early each morning so she could sit on the bedroom floor, watching her sleep. Mel liked waking her gently and watching her sit up in bed in her little pyjamas, rubbing the sleep from her eyes as she focused on her surroundings, her hair loose and tangled. She loved brushing her hair after she'd been in the shower and inhaling the aroma of the shampoo she had bought her, cherry blossom and almond.

Mel was surprised how easy it was to slip into a routine of caring for Cassie and rearranging her day around her needs outside of school.

'What would you like for breakfast today, Cassie?' Mel asked.

Cassie beamed. 'My favourite please.'

Carter made a noise as if he was clearing his throat. He nodded, indicating he would like to speak to Mel in another room.

'Pancakes it is. I'll just have a word with Carter and then I'll make them, okay?'

Carter was paced across the sitting room floor, hands on his waist. Annoyingly, he even looked handsome when he was angry.

'What the fuck, Mel? She's been here five days and you guys have a favourite breakfast menu.'

Mel felt her stomach tense. 'It's just banter, relax.'

'That's the thing. It's not just banter, and I think you know this yourself.'

'You're overreacting.'

'When does she leave, Mel?'

'I'll be speaking to the social worker today, leave it with me.' She felt sick. Cassie's mum was staying in hospital longer than expected and she had no idea how to break this news to Carter without a scene. 'You know, if you stopped overthinking and just saw her as a child who needs a temporary place to stay, you might feel differently. You're an adult, Carter. How do you think your rudeness impacts her when she is already so alone on the world? She's five years old for God's sake. And she is going home when her mum is well enough. I've not kidnapped her, so stop being so dramatic.'

His shoulders dropped and she knew for now at least, she had a reprieve. 'Fair point. You must understand how hard this is for me though, Mel. I'm not deliberately being horrible. I have two concerns. The first being that you're too attached to her, and the second is that despite how it may look I'm afraid to get attached too. She's leaving soon and then what happens? I mean you're getting up early to watch her sleep, for God's sake.'

Mel flushed, embarrassed that he saw through her so easily. 'You can speak to Cassie and interact without getting attached, you know.'

Carter raised his eyebrows. 'She reminds me too much of Ella. I can't do it,' he said.

Mel looked away. 'I know, but she's older than Ella was, so it's different. And she's funny and clever, and—'

'And exactly my point Mel. You're already overly attached to her. Realistically, what happens when she leaves? I'm worried this is all going to trigger the past trauma. While Cassie is here, you're distracted and busy, but once she's gone...' He reached out a hand and then pulled back.

Silence filled the space where reassuring words should have.

'I'd better get her ready for school and sort myself for work,' Mel said.

'Have a good day.' Carter kissed her and relief flooded through her when he left the house. It was no good putting this off any longer, she would have to tell him tonight that Ella needed to stay another few weeks.

Mel cooked Thai green curry with an entrée of spring rolls. When Carter walked through the door she reached straight into the fridge and took out a cold beer for him.

'Something smells good. Fishy, but good,' he said.

'Here you go.' Mel handed him the beer and a plate of spring rolls with dipping sauce. 'Curry will be ready in thirty minutes, but I'm going to get Cassie into bed so we can have to some time to ourselves.' Mel hoped that if he saw how easy this could be, he might react better.

'That was delicious.' Carter sat back in his chair with a smile on his face and his eyes closed. Mel was aware of the television muttering on in the background and her heart beating in her ears. She walked to the fridge and poured herself a white wine.

'It's not like you to drink on a work night. Tough day?'

'Something like that. I spoke to the social worker today.' She swallowed another mouthful of wine, noting Carter tensing as he sat upright.

'Apparently, there were some complications with the operation.'

He stood up and walked towards the window as if he did not want to hear anymore, hands pushed in trouser pockets.

Mel kept talking. 'Cassie's mum is going to be in hospital for another few weeks at least and then there's her recovery. She won't be well enough to have Cassie home at first.'

'I hope you told the social worker that they would need to place Cassie elsewhere.'

'Well, no. I mean, I wanted to talk to you about it.'

'That's what all this was about?' He waved him arm towards the table. 'You were trying to butter me up before we had this talk.'

Mel bit her lip a little too hard. She tasted the metallic bitterness of her own blood. 'Actually, I just wanted to spend a nice evening with my husband, but it seems that's too much to ask.' She was clutching at straws and she knew it.

'No. You're not playing victim, Mel. This is not okay. It's not healthy. I think Cassie is a lovely kid, but I really don't want her here another month or however long it stretches out to be.'

'Carter, please.'

'If you'd bothered to ask me in the beginning, we wouldn't be having this conversation because Cassie wouldn't be in the house right now, and everything would be fine. It beats me how we ended up with her in the first place. I thought social services were shit-hot on checking people out before putting kids with them.'

'We're already cleared to work with kids. And because we've finished the fostering process, it was pretty straight forward.'

'Except I'd not been consulted,' he said.

'I thought you wouldn't mind.'

'Well, I'm calling closure on this whole thing. I'm sorry, Mel. I know that's not what you want to hear, but it's for the best and please don't try to change my mind because this topic is no longer open for discussion.'

CHAPTER 28

MEL

Cassie was eating her breakfast when Carter walked into the kitchen. Mel busied herself to avoid looking at him. He poured himself a coffee and stood next to her.

'Do you plan on talking to me at all today?' he asked quietly.

She'd prefer not to. 'Of course, don't be silly. I'm just busy.'

'You were sleeping when I came to bed last night and I followed you up after ten minutes.' The accusation hung in the air.

'I was tired, I must have crashed.'

Carter turned to face her. 'Babe, I really am sorry.'

She nodded, afraid her voice might waver if she spoke.

'Don't shut me out Mel, that's what happened last time.'

He was right, but she couldn't help but feel angry and she wasn't sure if she was angry at herself for starting this in the first place or at Carter for ending it.

'I'm sorry too.'

'Don't let this drive a wedge between us.' He looked into her eyes.

She felt tears prickle. 'It won't. I'll sort things today. In fact, if you can hang around another five minutes, I'll go and call the social worker now. Obviously, I don't want Cassie to hear this.'

Mel sat on the bed and closed her eyes. The smell of lavender from the lava stones soothed her, but only slightly. She now had to break the news to Cassie that she would not be coming back here after school, she would instead be going to live with a stranger. It felt so wrong. She forced herself down the stairs and into the kitchen.

'All sorted?' Carter asked, and it took all of her restraint not to scream or slam something down on the bench.

'Well—Cassie is going home to a stranger tonight, so I guess it's *sorted*.' There was no hiding the hurt she felt.

'Ouch. So, l may have worded that insensitively. I didn't mean it to sound so ruthless.' He had the decency to look at the floor.

She continued to wipe the work surface that was already clean and now her hands would smell of mandarin and lime disinfectant for the rest of the morning.

Mel sat down next to Cassie as soon as Carter left for work.

'Cassie, I have something to tell you.'

'What is it?' she asked with her big brown eyes, so innocent and trusting.

'Well, you know how your mum is in hospital...' Her voice wobbled, and she cleared her throat. 'The thing is, when you came to stay with me, with us, you were only supposed to be here for a few days.'

'I like it here,' she said, smiling and Mel wished she wouldn't. This was harder than she'd anticipated.

'I know, Cass, and I've loved having you here, but because we don't know when your mum will be home, Cheryl, your social worker has found you a new home to stay at.' There, she'd said it.

'No! I don't want to go to another home, Miss. I like being here with you.'

It took everything within Mel not to break down and hold on to Cassie for dear life. Instead, she flowered up the new house move with a promise of games she knew Cassie loved. She would go out and buy them herself if it put a smile on her face. By the time they'd finished talking, Cassie had huffily accepted the situation and Mel had never felt so horrible as she did right now.

The rest of the day passed slowly. Mel waited for the social worker, who was coming fifteen minutes after school closed. Cassie sat at a table colouring in. She's been quiet all day, which was unlike her. Mel didn't blame her for being angry, but it certainly wasn't easing her guilt. When Cassie talked to the social worker, Mel said goodbye and excused herself. She couldn't stand to watch her go for fear that she would shout after them and tell them that she'd made a mistake.

She went for a walk along the seafront after work, not ready to face going home. The smell of the salty air was familiar and grounding. It made her think of Christmas and family times from when she was young, and it filled her with both sadness and happiness. Yin and Yang memories.

'Cheer up, it might never happen,' a man said as he walked towards her.

'It already did,' she replied, solemnly.

'I'm sorry, love. I was only messing with you. I hope everything's okay.'

She thought about his words as she walked on. She was being dramatic. Compared to what she had been through in the past, everything *was* okay. When she replayed the past three plus years, the loss of Ella, her struggle with mental health, he breakdown of her marriage, things were more than okay. Cassie wasn't her responsibility, she didn't have rescue her. The fact that she'd gone ahead with having her in the home without Carter's consent suddenly made her feel terrible. He would never do anything like that to her.'

'I owe you a huge apology,' she said to Carter as soon as she walked into the house. 'I should never have invited Cassie here without discussing it with you first. I can't even explain what came over me. I just saw a little girl who needed help and when I was asked to step in, it felt like it was the right thing to do.'

'Babe, it's okay. She's safe and she will be well cared for where she is. Let's just put this behind us.'

'Thank God it's almost the weekend. I'm exhausted,' Mel said.

'I wondered if this thing with Cassie was because Ari is having a baby?'

Mel paused rather than react. Honesty was better than denial. 'I admit that my world rocked a little when my sis announced her baby news, but I'm happy for them, really I am, and this thing with Cassie was nothing to do with Ari being pregnant.'

'I've been thinking about us having a night or two away. We could leave tomorrow and come home Sunday. What do you think?'

She was glad he had changed the subject. 'Where would we go?'

'I thought we could go to Yorkshire. Walk around the dales, eat some Yorkshire puddings and Eccles cakes.'

Mel laughed. 'Not together, I hope.' She stuck her fingers down her throat and did a mock gag. 'Okay, let's go. Fresh start and all that. The break will be nice, and I could do with some new scenery. This place gets stifling after a while.'

CHAPTER 29

—·—

MEL

After checking into the hotel in Ilkley, Mel and Carter drove onto the moors to walk to the famous Cow and Calf rocks.

Mel's boots crunched over the ground beneath her as she inhaled the woody smell of heather that was penetrating the moors. Fog hovered in the air as if the earth had been breathing too heavy.

'According to local legend,' Mel read from a leaflet to Carter behind her, 'the Calf was split from the Cow when the giant Rombald was fleeing an enemy and stamped on the rock as he leapt across the valley. The enemy, it is rumoured, was his angry wife. She dropped the stones held in her skirt to form the local rock formation The Skirtful of Stones.'

'It feels like we could walk forever on these Ilkley moors, but I'm not sure I'd want to be driving across here at night,' Carter said as he bit into a pork pie he pulled from his jacket pocket. 'My God, these are good,' he mumbled with a mouth full.

'It says here a fog often descends across the moors and people can get lost and drive off the road.' Mel felt that it was an eerie enough place during the day, let alone at night.

'We'll give that a miss. Speaking of fog and night-time, we should be making our way off these moors babe,' Carter said and he made an about turn and headed back to the car.

They were staying at Bistro Pierre, a French restaurant and boutique hotel. The restaurant was large and open, with pine floors and wall cladding and a vast white ceiling. Old pictures hung on the wall giving it a mixture of old and new. Tables were spaced out enough to not feel as if you were eating with strangers and Mel liked that.

'You look gorgeous,' Carter said as they sat opposite each other. She was wearing a simple fitted black dress and heels.

She smiled. 'You're easy pleased.'

He pushed a fork towards her. 'Here, try some of my tortellini.'

'No thanks. Wild boar is not really my thing.'

He laughed. 'You know it's just pork, right?'

'Erm, yes of course.' She blushed.

'You really didn't? What did you think boar was?'

She shrugged. 'Just some ugly beasts that run around forests.'

'Pretty good description of the locals.'

She swatted him. 'Shut up, or you'll get thumped.'

He smiled and silently mouthed 'I was joking' to her. 'Maybe we could buy a gift for your sister now that they know they're having a boy.

'Yeah, that would be nice,' Mel said. 'I wanted to buy her one of those baby swings that rock and play music.'

'Maybe we could buy two,' Carter said as he took a swig of his beer. His cheeks flushed, eyes twinkling.

'She's not having twins.'

'We could keep one for when we have another,' Carter said.

Mel was aware that her mouth was slack. She had not expected this turn in conversation.

'How would you feel about a baby?' he asked.

She inhaled sharply, emotions swirling within her. 'A baby.' The words fell off her tongue like jelly and the sound came out barely more than a whisper.

'I know it would be a big thing for both of us. But seeing you with Cassie, it was like we were there again, only it was the wrong child.' His eyes filled with sadness. 'I saw you light up again and I loved seeing you that happy, Mel. I just want it to be our story.'

Hope flooded through her, followed by fear. 'I don't know. I mean, of course I want a baby, a child, but I'm just not sure I could ever go through something like that again.'

'What happened would never happen again. It was a one in a million kind of thing, Mel. Imagine, me you and a baby. It would be different next time.'

'I can see that, and I want to believe you, but then I can also see me being overprotective and anxious.'

'We would work through that together.'

Mel chewed the inside of her cheek and pushed her hair behind her ear. A bubble of excitement was growing inside her. 'You really think we should?'

'I do. I really do.' He grabbed her hand and held it while looking at her. 'What do you think?'

'Can we talk more tomorrow? I want to say yes, but I need time to think about it.'

'Of course, there's no pressure and there's no rush, babe.'

Mel looked around the room at the people eating. There were several couples, a woman sat on her own, and two families with children. She tried to picture them with another child, but could only see Ella.

'Do you think about us with another child?' she asked as she pushed some couscous around her plate, distracted and no longer hungry.

'Yes, of course I do,' Carter said.

'What do you see?'

'What do you mean?' He furrowed his brow in confusion.

'I mean do you see us with one child, or two? Do you see a girl or a boy?'

'I'm not sure I've thought that specifically about it, to be honest. I just see us with a family. I want to come home to the sound of laughter and little voices and more than anything, I want to hear the word "Daddy" when I walk through the door.'

Mel felt her heart lurch. She wanted to hear that word too. And more, to have someone call her mummy. 'Okay, that's long enough thinking. Let's do it. Let's have another baby.' She put her hand on her chest, as if checking she was still there. 'I can't believe I've just said that out loud but again, yes I do want to try for a baby.' The more the words circled around her head, the better they sounded.

'Are you sure? You don't need time?' Carter asked.

'What would I be waiting on?' Mel asked, not waiting on a reply. 'No. I know what I want now. Also, it might take time so...' She smiled. 'Let's just do this.'

'And the fostering?'

'Well, let's see what happens over the next 6 months. I'm not sure we would manage a child of our own as well as fostering, so for now I would say it's on hold, if that's okay with you?'

'I think that's a wise decision and I also think this calls for a celebration.' Carter jumped up and came back with an ice bucket, champagne, and glasses. He popped the cork and Mel cringed as everyone turned to look at them.

'How embarrassing. You could have saved that for our room. Everybody's looking.'

'I don't care. Let them look.' Carter poured their drinks.

They tipped glasses and smiled. 'Cheers,' she said as they both toasted to their future. A new future that would hopefully include a baby.

CHAPTER 30

– · –

CARTER

Carter finally found a parking space so Mel could trawl through the shops, something he was not looking forward to. He ducked into the butcher's while Mel paid for parking, then presented her with his purchase.

'Here you go.' He handed Mel a huge sausage role.

'Why would I want to eat one of these? I never eat sausage rolls.'

He chuckled at the confused look on her face. 'They're famous! Everyone that visits Ilkley tries one.'

'They do? Are you sure, Carter?' She raised one eyebrow.

'Yes, so give it a try and we'll walk along the river before we hit the shops.'

They walked past families out on a stroll. There were people fishing, kids on bikes, and dogs chasing balls on the grass.

'Do you think that could be us soon?' Mel asked.

'I sure do.' Carter put his arm around her and kissed her. 'You will tell me if you change your mind? This has to be something we both want.'

'I do want it, but I think it's best we don't mention it to anyone else. I can't be done with expectant looks every month and those ominous questions about how I feel,' Mel said. 'It's a lot of pressure and I'm still finding my way through this so the less people know, the better. Our secret, right?'

'Our secret. And for what it's worth I think that's wise. I love your mum, but she can be a bit intense, and she'd be forever checking up on you.'

'That's exactly what I mean,' Mel laughed.

Carter looked at her and felt such happiness that they were back in this space. After Ella died, Mel had shut him out. She moved back to her mum's, saying she couldn't stand to be surrounded by memories and then she refused to talk to him or answer his calls. He'd almost given up hope until they met up at the graveside and he liked to think that Ella had played a part in that somehow.

'Just think, with your sis having her baby, how cool would it be to have our kids growing up together?'

'That would be so good, *but* I don't want to start thinking like that because it will only lead to expectation, and I don't want us to be disappointed.'

'Sorry. I'm getting carried away. I promise, aside from buying you the vitamins you need, I won't keep going on about it.'

'I still feel nervous.' Mel paused. 'Do you think it's disrespectful to Ella, us wanting another baby?'

Carter stopped and faced her. 'Mel, if we had ten kids we would never forget Ella. She will always be part of our lives and she will be part of our future children's as well.' He hugged her and kissed her forehead.

She nodded and smiled. 'Let's go shopping for my nephew.'

They linked hands and walked along the river towards the town centre, lost in ther bubble of future hopes and dreams.

CHAPTER 31

— · —

MEL

Mel looked at her Checklist: balloons, ribbon, nappies, a variety of different chocolate bars, and then food to collect on the way. It was the day of Ari's baby shower and there were going be around thirty people at her mum's house. The baby, a boy, was due to arrive in four weeks' time.

'Jade, can you grab that gift off the chair on the way out please?' Mel asked.

'What the hell is it?' Jade's head barely visible behind the wrapped gift and enormous blue bow.

'Baby swing, one of this singing dancing ones. Anything that gives a parent five minutes peace is worth its weight in gold.' Mel wondered if she would be buying one of her own soon.

'This baby is going to be so spoilt,' said Jade. 'And rightly so.'

'As long as the Mumma-to-be enjoys the baby shower, that's all that matters. It's actually more stressful arranging a baby shower than I thought it would be.'

Four hours later, her mum's conservatory and garden looked like a dishevelled baby photo shoot. There were streamers everywhere, nappies piled up in a corner and paper plates all over the grass after a gust of wind sent them airborne. The smell of chocolate lingered in the air.

'It's been a beautiful afternoon, darling. You did your sister proud,' Grace said.

'I got a video of the boys eating the melted snickers off the nappies. That was too funny.' Mel scrolled through her camera to show her mum.

'Oh, I am whacked,' Ari said as she heaved her baby bump into a chair. A whiff of talcum powder followed her. 'Thank you both so much. And thanks Mum for letting us take over your house. It's been great and I'm blown away with all the gifts.'

'Baby is not going to need any clothes until he is about one.' Grace smiled.

'Yes, we just need him to make an appearance now. It feels like I've been pregnant forever.' Ari rubbed her stomach and shifted uncomfortably in the chair.

'I remember those days. Feet under ribs and elbows digging in.' Mel said, remembering. Silence fell like a blanket, smothering the conversation so Mel made an effort to switch the mood. 'How amazing will Christmas be with him here!'

'It absolutely will, and I can't wait.' Grace smiled at her girls.

Three weeks later, one full week before his due date, baby Tate entered the world weighing seven pounds exactly. Mel walked onto the maternity ward, pushing away the memories that surfaced like corks as she scanned the rooms looking for her sister.

'How are you?' Mel gushed as she wrapped her arms around her sister. 'Oh my, look at him. Just look at him.' This perfect little human was lying in a cot dressed in a white velour babygrow. He was wearing a little beanie with his name embroidered on it, his dark hair poking out from underneath. Long dark lashes grazed his porcelain skin, and his little pink lips were like rosebuds. 'My God, he's beautiful, Ari.' Mel felt a lurch inside and a desperation to hold a child of her own again. For a moment Mel swam in a sea of memories as she brushed the silky skin of his cheek with her finger.

'Isn't he! I've barely shut my eyes since he was born because I just keep staring at him. His perfect little fingers and nails and just—well, I can't believe he's ours,' Ari said.

'Where is Jay?'

'He went home to bring me some clothes so I can freshen up. Everything happened quickly and my plan sort of went out of the window.'

'How bad was the labour?' Mel asked.

'Just like everyone says, as soon as you see your baby you forget about it. It's weird, you're in agony but you also know what you will have at the end of it. There's this thing inside that takes over. Inner primal strength you don't even know is there until it's needed.'

'It's crazy, isn't it? As soon as you look at your baby it becomes a memory, and you know you would do it all again in a heartbeat.'

Ari reached out for her hand. 'Are you okay? This must be hard for you, Mel.'

'I'm fine, sis,' Mel said gently. 'I've had seven months or so to get used to it. I am thrilled for you both. There's no better gift in the world than a baby and this little one is just beautiful.' Mel stroked Tate's face and smiled.

'It means such a lot to hear you say that, Mel.'

'Where's my grandson?' echoed down the corridor and they both burst out laughing as Grace entered the room laden with balloon and presents.

CHAPTER 32

— · —

MEL

Mel stood in the schoolyard with her coat zipped up, a hat on, and she stamped her feet on the ground in a bid to keep warm. It should be illegal to be on yard duty in this weather. The kids didn't seem to feel it as they ran around. She, on the other hand, was freezing as wind cut into her like a knife. The sky hung heavy with rain above her. It made her yearn for the smell of clean bedsheets and her comfortable mattress. She looked at her watch and waited for the buzzer. The children lined up and she ducked into the staff room to dump her coat.

Jules passed her room. 'You look a bit peaky this morning, Miss.'

'It's bloody freezing outside, I'm still thawing out.'

'Coffee at afternoon break?'

'See you then. I think I need it. I'm shattered and it's not even eleven am.'

The lunch bell rang, and once Mel had dispersed the children into the canteen, she walked into the staff room and slumped into a chair.

'We've got another four weeks until Christmas break,' Tom the Year Four teacher jibed.

'Here you go, this will wake you up.' Jules said as she wafted a cup of coffee under Mel's nose like smelling salts.

Mel took the coffee and put it on the side table next to her. 'How's your morning been?' she asked Jules.

'Busy as per. What about you? How are you?'

'Okay, I guess. I'm just not feeling it today. Maybe I slept bad.'

'Well, don't stay back tonight. Go straight home and take it easy,' Jules said.

Mel smiled. 'Yes, mother.'

Jules dug her in the ribs. 'I'm just looking out for you.'

'I know my friend, and I appreciate it. This term must have been tougher than I thought.' Mel said as she closed her eyes that were fighting to stay open.

That night Carter came home with their usual Wednesday night take-out, one green curry with rice and one Pad Thai. Mel plated the food and they sat down to eat.

'You're just pushing that around your plate. Are you not hungry?' Carter asked.

'I've felt a bit off all day. There are kids off school with different viruses, so no doubt I'm getting one of them. The perks of being a teacher.' Mel rolled her eyes. 'I might just get an early night. I've got two more days to put in before the weekend.'

'Okay. Can I get you anything?'

'No, I'm fine, I'm just wiped out.'

The next morning Mel could barely put one foot in front of the other, she was so exhausted. She called in sick and crawled back into bed, where she stayed until lunchtime.

She was lying on the sofa with the fire on when Carter came in from work just after six pm. 'It's so nice in here, the wind is icy today. How are you feeling, babe?' He sat on the chair opposite her with a slight grin on his face.

'Well, I've felt worse, but I'm also not great. I think I might have the flu. I'm not sure why you're grinning though. It's not funny, Carter.' He laughed and she closed her eyes in annoyance. She couldn't be bothered with him right now. 'I'm tired, and not in the mood.'

'I bought you something though.' he teased.

'What do you mean?' He was irritating her, and she wished he would go busy himself with something.

'Keep your eyes closed and put your hands out.'

She sighed and did as he said. She felt a long box in her hands. It was light and she was trying to guess what it could be when he interrupted her thoughts.

'Open your eyes, then.'

She looked at her hands. 'You bought me a pregnancy test, that's just—' Her brain started working overtime. 'You think I'm pregnant?'

'All I know is the last time you were this tired and off your favourite food, you were pregnant.' Expectation danced in his eyes.

Her stomach flipped at the thoughts running through her head. It would be the best and most worrying thing ever. 'You think I should wait until tomorrow morning?'

'Do you want to wait that long? I know I don't,' he said.

Ten minutes later, they looked at the timer on Mel's phone. The test was face down. 'I can't bear it,' she said. 'I have so many conflicting emotions right now.'

'What are you feeling?'

'Excitement to the point of wanting to cry. Fear and worry to the point of hoping I'm not, but obviously, I want to be.'

'We love each other, we have a comfortable life, so there's nothing to worry *or* fear,' Carter reached her hand. 'We've got this babe.'

'You know exactly what I would worry about, though. I have reason for that,' Mel said.

'Well, what say we find out if there's anything to worry about before you actually start worrying.' Carter smiled at her and she envied his view on life. He was so practical. She wished she could be more like him.

'Okay. Can you look at it though?' Her insides churned like she was riding the waves of a storm.

Mel watched Carter pick the test up as if she were viewing the scene in slow motion, the only sound her heartbeat reverberating in her ears.

'Let me see it.' She grabbed for it suddenly. There were two lines. 'I'm pregnant!' She looked at Carter, finding his eyes glossy. 'I'm pregnant,' she repeated.

'Yes, babe. You are and we're going to have a baby.' Carter hugged her as tears of happiness, relief, and grief flowed out of her.

'My God, it's real.' She picked up the stick again. 'It's really happening. How did you know? It hadn't even crossed my mind.'

'When you couldn't eat your favourite Thai, I knew that something was up.'

'I feel like I'm dreaming with my eyes open. I haven't even asked how you feel.' Mel said.

'I'm ecstatic babe. I've wanted this for so long. I really couldn't be happier.'

That night, Mel lay in bed with her hands on her stomach, already feeling protective over the life growing inside her. She silently prayed to whoever was listening to not take this child from them and to keep their baby safe.

CHAPTER 33

— • —

GRACE

Grace stood in front of the mirror examining the wrinkles on her face and the greying of her hair that she hid beneath the blonde dye.

'Dear God, my neck looks like a turkey,' she whispered to herself. Aging was a funny process. You're young and carefree one day, and next minute you look at a reflection of yourself in the mirror trying to recognise your own face.

She sighed. For a second, she understood how easy it would be for people to step into that world of filler and Botox. The last time they had been to Edinburgh shopping, she had noticed groups of young women, all looking like clones of each other. They looked beautiful, but she wondered what would happen as they got older and other parts of their body started to show aging. You would need a bottomless pit of money. She turned away from the mirror to avoid the internal torture of analysing each wrinkle. Grace squirted her favourite perfume because it always put a smile on her face.

You're alive and well, you old fool, and you can't expect to look like you did thirty years ago, she said to herself sternly as she made her way downstairs.

'What are you cooking? It smells like a bakery in here,' Grace asked John as she inhaled the aroma of mixed spices and oranges.

'Well, Christmas is just a couple of days away,' said John, 'so I thought I would make some mince pies. Now that Ari is gluten free, I am making her an orange and almond cake. And while I'm busy, I thought I would prepare a nice meal for us for this evening.'

'That's so kind of you, darling, and very brave taking on all of that baking and cooking. I'm meeting the girls and Tate at twelve, but I should be back around two. Are you sure you don't want to join us? I feel bad leaving you slaving away in the kitchen.' She chuckled. 'But I also have to admit there's a part of me likes it.'

'No, I'm fine. You have a lovely time with your girls and Tate, and I'll see you later.' He was acting a little strange and Grace wondered if he was having second thoughts about them living together.

'Are you okay, John?'

He walked over to her and gently took hold of both her hands, sending a flurry of flour to the floor. 'I am perfectly fine my dear, in fact I am positively happy.'

He really was acting strange. 'Okay,' Grace laughed, 'well I'm off out now and I will leave you to your cooking.' She walked out of the house feeling as if something was slightly off, but couldn't quite put her finger on what it was.

Mel and Ari were sitting in front of the window at The Little Tea House. It reminded Grace of when they were small. She would watch them play and listen to their innocent chatter and vivid imaginations running wild. It seemed only a few breaths since they were that small, and yet here they were, both married women.

Time is so precious and wasted on worrying about things out of our control, Grace thought to herself as she got out of the car and made her way into the café.

'Mum. You look lovely,' Mel said.

'Thank you, sweetheart. And you both look gorgeous as always,' she said as she hugged her girls. 'And on a totally different note, this lunch was very impromptu, but a lovely idea all the same.' Grace turned to Tate, who sat in his stroller, thrashing around a toy attached to the handle. He gave her a grin and showed off his six teeth. 'How's my favourite gorgeous boy?' she asked. He screwed his face up and then started giggling.

'He can stay in there, otherwise there will be hell on Earth in here,' Ari said, smiling. 'Won't there be, you little terror? I can't leave this one for two seconds and he's pulling a plant over or hiding something, aren't you?' She squeezed his face, and he blew a raspberry at her.

'Can we order food? The smells wafting around this place are making me hungry,' Grace asked.

'I'll go and order and then there's something I need to ask you both.' Mel stood up and made her way to the counter.

'Is she okay?' Grace asked Ari.

'I think so. She's not said anything to make me think that things aren't okay.'

Mel sat down and smiled at them both.

'So...'Ari said. 'What do you want to ask us?'

She handed them both a card. Grace looked at Ari, bemused and they opened their cards together. Grace read the words:

Dear Mum, please keep the following date free (approx.) Tenth July 2008, I really love you to be there when your grandchild is born. Love Mel & Carter. Xx

'Oh, my goodness. You're pregnant!' Grace gasped and tears rolled down her face as they all hugged.

'You're going to get a cousin, Tate!' Ari squealed and Tate looked around in confusion, no doubt wondering what all the fuss was about. 'This is amazing news, Mel. The kids can grow up together and they'll be so close.'

'Do you feel okay, darling?' Grace asked.

'I'm tired, but apart from that I'm okay. I'm a bit anxious though. You know, about things going wrong.'

'That's understandable. You're young and healthy though, and I'm sure things will be fine, but it's always

nerve wracking until you pass the twelve-week stage.'
Ari said.

'It's not just about the pregnancy though, it's—'

Grace put her hand on Mel's. 'Darling, things will
be different this time and I'm sure you can speak to
your midwife and doctor about your worries. They
will understand and be able to reassure you.'

'How excited is Carter?' Ari asked.

Mel laughed. 'Oh, you know him. He knew I was
pregnant before I did. I thought I was coming down
with something from one of the kids from school.
Carter told me he'd bought me a present and it turned
out it was a pregnancy test.'

'How many weeks pregnant are you?'

'Nine weeks. We were going to wait until Christmas
day to tell you, but we couldn't keep it a secret any
longer.'

'It's amazing news, darling and I'm so happy for you
both.'

An hour later, Grace almost floated out of the café.
She punched a number into her mobile. 'John. It's
me. I have the most wonderful news, so I'm going to
pick up a bottle of champagne.'

'I already have a bottle chilling, darling.'

'You do?' Her mind raced a thousand miles per hour, and she wondered how he knew before her. 'Did Mel tell you?'

'Tell me what?'

'That she's pregnant,' Grace said.

'She is? Oh, that's wonderful.'

'I'm so confused. Why would you already have champagne chilling if you didn't know?'

'It's our anniversary. It's two years since we went on our first date,' John said.

Grace felt herself flush like a teenager. How sweet of him to remember. How awful that she didn't! 'Oh John, I'm sorry I forgot. That's why you're cooking us a meal.' No wonder he had been acting strange. 'I'll make it up to you.'

She called into the travel agents and booked a four-night trip to Jersey for March when the weather might be a bit kinder to them. She had all but forgotten how to make a fuss about these things. After you've been married for a while, the fanfare dies down to faint acknowledgement. She'd been on her own so long before John that it felt strange to celebrate like a young couple. She decided to buy him some handmade chocolates. They cost a small fortune but were worth it for a special occasion. John had a sweet tooth, so he would appreciate them.

'Good morning, Grace, how are you? It's not often I see you in here,' Lena said.

Lena was the owner of the chocolate shop and the biggest gossip for miles around.

'Hi, Lena. How on Earth do you manage to stay slim working in here? The smell is divine. I'd be at those chocolates all day long.'

'It loses its appeal after years, believe me. And then there's the fact I'd be out of business if I ate all of my profits, not to mention the waistline.' She pinched an imaginary inch and Grace was in awe of her figure for a woman in her late forties.

'I don't think I would ever get sick of them. Speaking of which, I'll take four of the pralines, two caramel, two lemon, two strawberry and you can choose another four of the best for me.'

'Special occasion?' Lena raised her eyebrow.

'You could say that.' Grace smiled and paid for her chocolates, determined not to give in to the rumour mill.

Grace sat across the table from John as he poured them both a glass of champagne. Grace watched the bubbles dance to the top of the glass and noted that John was wearing a little more aftershave than usual.

'To us,' she said, as they clinked glasses.

'To us.' John took a drink and then cleared his throat. 'Actually, us was something I wanted to talk to you about.'

She knew it. He was having doubts. Her stomach sank and she berated herself for telling him that she'd forgotten their anniversary. Maybe that was the straw that broke the camel's back.

'Okay.' Grace braced herself as she looked at John fidgeting. He was clearly uncomfortable with what he was about to say. Her insides knotted together.

'Who would have thought that when we went out for lunch two years ago we would be living together? I know when I moved in I said that life is short...'

'John, if you're having second thoughts—' Grace interrupted.

'Grace. Please, let me finish. I said that life was short, and I meant it. That is why...' John moved off the chair and knelt on the floor in front of her. 'That is why I would like to ask you if you would do me the honour of becoming my wife?'

Grace looked at him as he waited for her reply. She was stunned. She'd thought he wanted to move out, and here he was proposing.

'Grace. Can you put me out of my misery here before my knee gives way?'

She burst out laughing. 'Yes! Yes, I will marry you.' She couldn't quite believe she was saying those words out loud, but she just had, and now he was slipping a ring on her finger.

'Could you help me up?' he asked, and they both burst out laughing. John kissed her, hugged her, chattered about having a small party with the family.

Grace watched this as if it were in slow motion. She felt as if she had betrayed Tom and she wondered how the girls would take the news. She loved John and they got along well and enjoyed each other's company, but marriage was not something she'd thought about.

'I think you should phone the girls.' John was pouring them another glass of champagne.

'Did they know about this?' she asked.

'Hell, no. I was terrified they might not agree.'

Her stomach sank. 'Don't be silly, I'm sure they'll be happy for us.' She prayed that they would be as she facetimed them both.

Ari was cleaning the kitchen after getting Tate to sleep and Mel and Carter were lying on the sofa in front of a toasty fire.

'What's up, Mum?' Ari asked as she propped the phone up and wiped benches. Tate's cry echoed from upstairs, and she rolled her eyes. 'Your turn, Jay. Gosh, your fire looks ace, sis. I bet you don't want to move from that sofa.'

Mel smiled. 'Got it in one.'

John came in behind Grace and waved and said hello to everyone. He nudged Grace, always awkward on video. 'Go on, then.'

'Go on what?' Mel asked.

'That's why I'm calling you both.' She felt herself flush and could have cheerfully choked John for forcing her to say it. 'John proposed to me tonight.' She watched their expressions change from surprise to radiant smiles.

'Oh my! Congratulations, Mum, that's fantastic!' Mel said.

'I'm so happy for you,' both girls chimed.

'You really don't mind?' Grace asked, genuinely concerned.

'Mum, we were the ones telling you to get out there and meet someone for long enough. Of course we don't mind, do we Mel?' Ari said.

Grace felt her body relax as soon as she ended the call. 'Well, that was easier than I thought it would be,' Grace said as she turned to John.

'Yes, I have to say they were amazing and very supportive. Now we have their blessing we can decide when and where we will get married.'

'Oh, I'd not even thought about it. Something quiet and fuss free will be nice.'

'How about somewhere abroad?' John suggested.

'Oh no, John, I'd want the girls and their families there.'

'I meant all of us, Grace. I know you'd never marry without the girls there and I would never ask you to.'

'Let's worry about that after Christmas. There's no rush and we would need to wait on the baby arriving before we could even consider going overseas for a wedding. It does sound idyllic though,' Grace said.

Grace looked down at her ring and smiled to herself. She would call her friends tomorrow and knew what Karen would say before she spoke to her. *'Life's too short to be lonely, Grace and you need to grab happiness whenever you can.'*

CHAPTER 34

—·—

MEL

Mel walked into her classroom and wrinkled her nose at the smell. She picked up the bin to find a half-eaten apple core that had festered over the weekend. *Damn those cleaners! She picked the bag out of the bin and walked outside to the bin.*

'Hi Miss,' several voices yelled out. Mel gave a quick wave and walked as quickly as her legs would carry her back into the classroom for some moments of quiet before the Monday morning bell rang.

She sat at her desk and ran her finger over the grainy wood, etched with years of dirt and small fingerprints, and felt mixed emotions about her last week at work. After the holidays, a relief teacher would stand in her place; sit in this very chair. The children would greet her good morning and it made Mel feel protective of her room, a space she had created and honed to make the children feel welcome and safe. It felt like hers and hers alone, its smell a mixture of disinfectant and pencil shavings.

Her eyes landed on a note from Jules that lay on top of a pile of books. *I'm on yard duty, so I will see you at break time.* Mel loved the friendship she had with Jules, who always managed to sum up a person or situation with so few words and usually most of those words would involve foul language. Jules was also incredibly kind and caring and had the biggest heart. Mel sent her a text asking her to come to her classroom at breaktime. She had no desire to heave her heavy body upstairs to the staff room unless absolutely necessary.

'So, how are you feeling about your six-week holiday before the baby arrives?' Jules asked.

'I can't wait to put these swollen ankles up on the sofa every day while I watch trashy TV and stuff my face with marshmallows and chocolate. Marshmallow craving aside I am looking forward to lazy mornings and me time before two become three.' *Again,* echoed in her head but she pushed down the wave of emotion that crashed about inside of her.

Jules laughed. 'I hope you are up for visitors. I'm definately going to miss you around this place.'

'Don't forget about me mind you!'

'No chance. I'll be knocking on your door and keeping you up to date on what's happening. I will even come armed with chocolate *covered* marshmallows.'

Mel placed her hand on her heart. 'The door is always open. In fact, you can have a key.' She laughed and dipped her hand into her desk drawer. 'Don't tell the kids,' she whispered quietly, before stuffing a marshmallow into her mouth.

On her last day at work, the children filed into her classroom with gifts for both her and the baby. Cassie brought blue and pink cupcakes and the children spent the morning watching movies, making cards and playing outside in the sunshine. Cassie was back in the care of her mum and she was thriving, and thankfully she never referenced the time she'd spent at Mel's house. It was almost as if had never happened.

'You're wanted in the staff room, Mel,' Dawn said.

Mel lifted herself out of her chair and walked into the staff room to the song *I Just Haven't Met You Yet* by Michael Bublé. Everyone clapped as Jules brought out a huge chocolate cake with edible pink and blue balloons on top.

'They're made of marshmallow,' Jules mouthed, smiling.

The head teacher Emily stood up and everyone hushed. 'Mel, we all wanted to wish you a very restful break and I personally want to thank you for an amazing year with your class. We will look forward to meeting baby whenever he or she arrives, and we've all contributed to a gift.'

'Thank you, Emily, and thank you all for being so supportive.' Mel said.

'Here you go, Mel.' Jules edged towards her with a huge parcel.

Mel unwrapped it and gasped. 'Oh, wow guys, this is amazing and beyond generous. Thank you so much.

Carter and I bought my sister one of these swings and they're amazing.'

'It rocks baby to sleep apparently, so we figured anything that might give you more sleep is a definite bonus.' Jules said.

'I'm going to have to do two trips home tonight, what with all the gifts the kids brought in.'

'I'll help Mel, we can load my car up and save you coming back.'

'Thanks Jules. Now what say I cut this cake and we all have a sugar fix before we face those excited kiddies again? Two hours and counting until that bell rings.'

CHAPTER 35

— • —

MEL

Mel watched the screen intently as the probe slid across her stomach. Her heart was in her throat. She gripped Carter's hand.

'You did the right thing coming in, Mrs Steadman. Baby is fine but it's always best to check these things if you're concerned,' the sonographer said.

'Sorry, I didn't mean to waste your time.'

'You didn't waste her time,' Carter said as he turned to her.

'Your husband's right, and maybe next time we see you, baby will be on the way to making an appearance.'

'Should we ask?' Mel looked at Carter.

'If you want to.'

'Can you tell us the sex of the baby? I know we're just a few weeks away, but I have this sudden desire to know.'

The sonographer smiled. 'You're having a baby girl, and everything looks just fine.'

Mel looked to Carter and bittersweet memories danced between them.

Carter squeezed her hand. 'Another princess, babe.'

Mel smiled and nodded. 'Another princess.'

Mel rubbed her swollen belly and mentally counted down the four weeks and three days that were left before their baby was due to make an appearance.

'I thought you might like a fruit smoothie.' Carter handed her a drink. The baby squirmed as if agreeing and Mel took a drink, savouring the icy coldness and the tartness of berries.

'I thought we could go and pick up the pram today, just in case this one decides to make an early appearance,' Mel said as she leaned forward and spoke to the life inside of her. 'I need to feel prepared. And besides, second babies can be unpredictable.'

In the car Mel sat quietly and Carter put his hand on tops of hers. 'Are you okay?'

'I was just wondering whether she will look like Ella.'

'She will look like her own little self.' He rubbed her hand reassuringly. 'Are we still going with the name we agreed on?'

'Ruby Mae Steadman,' Mel whispered with a smile. Ella's middle name had been Mae.

Mel couldn't stop looking at the pram. She gripped the handles and wheeled it back and forth a few times, imagining their tiny bundle all snug inside. Mel wished they had found out the sex sooner because the clothes they had were mostly white.

'Let's buy some pink outfits tomorrow,' she said.

'Don't we already have enough clothes to start up our own store?'

'Yes, but none are pink.'

'Fair point, and we can't have Ruby coming home in nothing less than pink. Are we going to tell anyone before the birth or are we still firm on a surprise? You know my parents will be desperate to rush out and buy girls' clothes from now until she's five.'

Mel laughed. 'Remember when your mum said she'd been shopping, and she turned up with three carrier bags full of clothes.'

'Yes, and I think my dad still remembers the bill.'

Mel braced herself for another contraction and reached for the gas and air. Her contractions had been three minutes apart when they'd arrived at hospital and that was four hours ago. She was now nine centimetres dilated and feeling exhausted.

'It won't be long now, babe, and then we will have our little princess in our arms safe and sound.'

Mel willed herself not to snap at Carter. She knew he meant well and what he said was true but when she felt as if she was being torn apart from the inside out, it did not help. And when was soon anyway? She felt like she'd been in labour far longer than the ten hours since she'd felt her first contraction.

The midwife Kerry cleared her throat. 'Just another check, Mel, to see if you're fully dilated yet. I'll make it as quick as I can.'

Kerry was a mum of two and she made Mel feel at ease. Mel tried to distract herself with thoughts of all of the things she would eat when this baby was born.

'You're a smidge off ten centimetres so tell me when you get the urge to push my lovely.'

'Can I do anything? Cold flannel? Water?' Carter asked. He had stress written all over his face.

'I think you've watched one too many episodes of *Call the Midwife*.' Kerry laughed and Mel wanted to laugh with them but the urge to push rippled through her body like a tsunami.

'Good, Mel. Keep going.' Kerry urged, while Mel gripped Carter's hand. 'Baby's head is crowning, another four good pushes and then I need you to stop pushing,' Kerry instructed.

The ring of fire. How could she have forgotten about it? Mel grabbed for the gas and air as she tried to breathe through the urge to push. She could hear

Carter and Kerry telling her what a great job she was doing and then suddenly the baby was out. After what felt like an eternity, Ruby let out a cry and the midwife placed her onto Mel's chest.

The rush of love was intoxicating and all Mel could do was stare at Ruby and stroke her body while tears of joy poured down her face. Carter was crying and trying to gently hug the both of them.

Carter cut the cord and then Mel was wheeled into the bathroom, where a bath had been run for her. She forgot all about her exhaustion as she lay there, beyond thankful their daughter had arrived safe and well.

Back in the delivery suite, she made herself comfortable in bed and looked at the crib.

'Welcome to the world, Ruby Mae Steadman. You are already loved more than you will ever know,' Mel said quietly.

'You were amazing, Mel. I'm so proud of you. If Ruby has half of your strength, she'll be a survivor. Oh, and she weighs seven pounds eight ounces,' Carter said.

'I can't wait to get home with her. Do you think they'll let us go today?' Mel asked.

'I hope not. You need to rest and get some sleep. You've been in labour for twelve or so hours.'

'How on Earth can I sleep? Look at her. Her tiny perfect fingernails, and tiny little ears, and her beautiful face and—'

Carter silenced her with a kiss. 'I get it. You're on a baby high.'

'You know, I read somewhere once that when you think you're done, as in exhausted and you want to give up, you're only at forty percent of what you are capable of achieving. I'm sure it was David Goggins that wrote that. I read his book. Anyway, it's true. I was beyond exhausted five hours ago, but I now feel more awake than I have in months.'

'I can't argue with that, because I've just witnessed it. On a different note, I think the midwife is coming back with some food for you and then you're moving to the ward.'

'Unless I'm allowed to go home.'

Carter raised his eyebrow. 'Can we compromise here? Will you at least stay in one night? I'd feel happier if you did.'

'Okay,' Mel said. 'One night, but we are coming home tomorrow. Can you do the honours of calling everyone and maybe ask them if they can wait until we are home before they visit. I know it will drive them crazy waiting, but it's only twenty-four hours. They've waited nine months so I'm sure they'll survive another day. Send them a picture though.'

'Of course, babe. Can I get you anything from the café?' Carter asked.

Mel shook her head as she stroked Ruby's cheek. 'I've got everything I need right here.'

CHAPTER 36

THREE YEARS LATER

Mel grabbed her car keys and checked that she had her purse in her bag. 'Come on, Ruby we have to go and buy a dress for Grandma's wedding,' she shouted.

Ruby ran down the hallway, breathless, her blue eyes gleaning with excitement. 'What colour?'

'I'm not sure, I guess we will ask Grandma that when we meet her at the train station.'

Ruby clapped her hands and walked towards the car. The morning air was still crisp, daffodil buds pushing through the soil. Mel liked this time of year as the country looked brighter and there was a change in peoples' mood as everyone clung to the hope of sunshine, late evenings and more time outdoors.

'Grandma, can I choose my dress?' Ruby asked as she rushed up to her.

Grace smiled. 'Of course you can, darling. You choose whichever dress you want.'

'Mum, don't give her too many options, otherwise you might regret that.'

The three of them stepped off the train into the hustle and bustle of Edinburgh station. The smell of food assaulted them from different angles.

'I'm hungry.' Ruby said, sniffing the air around her.

'You're always hungry, bub. Here have a banana and once we've bought you a dress, we will go for something to eat, okay?'

'Okay,' Ruby replied, although her face said it was far from okay, but she bit into the banana and was soon distracted by a bulldog puppy with a pink studded harness. 'Can we get a dog?'

'No Ruby, we can't get a dog.' Mel replied before pressing the traffic light button. The dog sniffed at Ruby's foot, and she burst into giggles and offered the dog some of her banana. The dog declined and Ruby shrugged her shoulders before pushing the remainder of the fruit into her mouth.

Ruby tried on six different dresses and settled for a navy-blue velvet dress with silk waist sash. It matched her eyes and made her creamy skin look almost lumi-nous.

'Are you happy with your choice?' Mel asked as she reached for her purse.

'Yes, Mummy. Ella loves it too.'

Mel and her mum locked eyes. 'Okay, well that's good.' Mel replied with hesitation.

She paid for the dress and handed Ruby the bag to carry. 'There you go, Ruby, your very own princess dress.'

Ruby twirled on the spot and then skipped to the door, bag in hand. 'I can't wait to show Dad my dress.'

'I can't wait to get on that plane to Cyprus, Mum,' Mel said. 'How are you feeling about the wedding? There's just under two weeks before we fly out there. Have the nerves started yet?'

'I know how many days and hours there are, darling. I keep a countdown app on my phone.'

'You did that yourself? Or did you ask Ari? Speaking of Ari, I forgot to ask her if she'd bought Tate an outfit yet, she was struggling to find one that she liked.'

'She did. It's very cute. He has pale blue shorts with a white short sleeve shirt, a little bow tie and braces. I told her it might be too cold for shorts in early April, but she insists he will be fine.'

'Ruby chose well then, their outfits will complement each other's.'

'It will be a lovely day and I wouldn't mind if the kids' outfits didn't match, I just want you all there with us.'

Mel squeezed her mum's hand. 'Let's go and get some food before Ruby pipes up again. I swear she has hollow legs. And then it's my turn to find something to wear. Brace yourself mum, you know how fussy I am so this could be a long day.' Mel jibed.

CHAPTER 37

— · —

MEL

As they flew into Larnaca, Tate and Ruby, who were sitting in the row behind them, became more animated. Mel turned her head to where her mum and John were in the row opposite.

'There's a part of me still can't believe this is real.' Grace said.

John squeezed her hand and then kissed it. 'I, for one, am pleased it is real.'

'Me too.' Grace smiled.

Mel smiled to herself. It seemed there was no age limit when it came to love.

The airport was an experience with two young children who were terribly excited to be on their first holiday overseas, and after a mad dash back to the plane for Tate's favourite toy they walked out of the airport.

'Welcome to Cyprus. My name is Andreas,' the concierge said as he guided them to the minibus and loaded luggage into the boot. 'I will be driving you to your hotel today.'

Tate and Ruby were ecstatic to see a herd of hundreds of goats on the drive to Nicosia. The goats flooded the road, a flurry of white, brown, and black as far as the eye could see.

'Oh, look one just had a poo,' Tate shouted.

'Tate!' Ari snapped.

Carter pursed his lips. 'Don't laugh.' Mel whispered. 'You'll only encourage Tate and Ari will not thank you for it. Carter silently pulled his finger along his mouth as if zipping it up.

The hotel was small compared to some of the others they had stopped off at, but that was precisely why Grace had chosen it, she said she wanted intimate and she could not have chosen a better venue. There was a private function room which was used for weddings and birthday parties, so it meant that they had some privacy from the rest of the hotel guests. The function room had whitewashed walls and marble floors with French doors that allowed sunlight to illuminate the room. The French doors led outside onto a patio and small garden area, with steps leading down to a private beach.

'It's beautiful! Mum. You hit gold with this hotel, and I doubt you could have found a better venue.'

'Thank you darling.' Grace replied.

'What's the plan for the next two days?' Mel asked.

'Well, today it's just the eight of us. Tomorrow Karen and Tim arrive at eleven am and then John's two friends get here late afternoon.'

'And the next day you get married.' Mel smiled.

'The next day I do indeed get married. How lucky am I to be in Cyprus with my beautiful family around me.

'It will be perfect mum.' Mel said.

The family spent the next day exploring the area and eating delicious Cypriot food with Karen, Tim, Gregg, and David. They ordered Cypriot Mezes which was a feast made up of dips, cold meats, olives, and breads, followed by calamari, kebabs, fish, and a variety of hot dishes that just kept coming. The smell of spices and sunshine hung in the air, and occasion-

ally the wind blew in the salty smell of the Mediter-
ranean.

Mel, Ari, and Ruby made their way to Grace's room
to have their hair styled while the boys looked after
Tate.

'Well, while you three are getting your hair done, I'll
go and put my dress on.' Grace said, as she exited out
of the stylist chair.

'Do you need any help, Mum?' Mel asked.

'No, darling. I will be fine, thanks.'

Twenty minutes later Grace walked back into the
room. Her cream dress fell just below the knee and it
was fitted but not clingy. The jacket lapel was edged
with a pale blue overlay. She was wearing a wide cream
brimmed hat with two blue feathers, stems crossed
and secured with a band of diamanté. Grace had
thought the hat over the top, but Mel and Ari had
insisted she buy it to finish off her outfit.

'Mum, you look drop dead gorgeous!' Ari said.

'I second that.' Mel echoed. 'John will be blown away when he sees you. That outfit looks even better than it did in the shop. You're stunning mum.'

Mel peaked her head into the function room. There was a centrepiece of frangipani and jasmine at each table and the room was in full bloom with large standing vases, overflowing with the blossoms. The heady smell of flowers was diluted by a gentle breeze carried through the French doors.

'I don't think I've ever seen anything as romantic,' Ari said, before she chased after Tate, who was making his way towards the sea.

'That kid is a handful,' Carter said with a smile on his face.

'Yeah, and I swear you love it,' Mel said.

'He's pretty funny with it, you've got to admit.'

'Don't let my sis hear you praising his naughty behaviour. She'll string you up. '

Ruby interrupted them after seeing a basket of lollies on the buffet table outside, and then Tate piped up that he'd already eaten one. Before a cascade of tears began, Mel ran outside and brought back two sweets, one for Ruby and one for Tate.

'But—'

Mel put her hand up and reached down to whisper in Ruby's ear. She could smell the sweet aroma of her apple shampoo. 'Shh. I sneaked you an extra sweet in my bag so you and Tate are even, but you have to wait until Grandma and John have been married, okay?'

Ruby smiled and looked at Tate. 'Okay, Mum,' she whispered before kissing Mel on the cheek. 'Ruby, come and stand with us. Granny will be here in a minute, and we have to take a seat and be very quiet while they are married.'

'We need a seat for Ella though and there's only three,' Ruby said.

Carter never felt prepared for these moments, even though they were frequent. Each time it knocked him, and he had to stop and take a minute before he responded.

'I'm sure we can sort something out,' he said in a bid to avoid a scene.

The marble floor announced the arrival of the bride, and everyone turned. Grace and John walked through the door together.

'They make a handsome couple, don't you think?' Carter said.

'They do.'

Carter turned to Mel, and he could see she was struggling to hold back the happy tears pooling in her eyes.

He placed his hand in hers affectionately.

After photographs, they all feasted on a buffet that kept increasing in size despite everyone tucking in heartily. Staff wandered around, offering up platters of food and the children had their own private party complete with buffet and children's entertainer.

Carter poured Mel a glass of champagne and handed it to her. 'Your mum looks radiant and very happy.'

'She really does,' Mel stated.

'Daddy, Daddy. Look at what I made!' Ruby came running towards them, showing a ladybird shaped balloon, Tate hot on her heels carrying what looked like a giraffe with short legs.

Carter looked around him and turned to Mel.

'We're pretty lucky, aren't we?'

'Yes. Yes we are.' Mel asked.

'We are in a beautiful country surrounded by close family, and we have our beautiful daughter who is a bundle of energy. Speaking of which...' Carter nodded to Ruby, who had ran to the courtyard and was now twirling with her arms out and laughing to herself.

'What are you doing, Ruby?' Carter asked.

'We're dancing with dragonflies, daddy. Me and Ella are dancing with dragonflies.' Ruby said as she twirled around and looked into the space that surrounded her as two dragonflies darted to and fro.

Carter looked at Mel and stood up with his hand outstretched. 'Do you want to go and dance?'

And that is exactly what they did. They danced and laughed, and Mel swore she saw a flash of red next to Ruby as she spun around with her arms in the air.

— · —

SUPPORT

If someone is in immediate danger, please call triple zero 000 (Australia) 999 (UK) or 112 (UK and Europe)

If you or someone you know is in need of support, please call Lifeline on 13 11 14 (Australia)

Australian Centre for Grief and Bereavement

Samaritans (UK) 116 123

thegoodgrieftrust.org (UK)

— · —

ABOUT LAURA

Laura was born in the UK and emigrated from North East England to Australia in 2011. Laura currently resides in Brisbane, QLD, where she runs her own counselling and training business.

To find out more about new releases please check out Laura's website:

www.lauraadams.author.com

Printed in Great Britain
by Amazon